Shadows Sing vol.2

Shadows Sing vol.2

Alyson M. Wilson

CONTENTS

CONTENTS

Pure Intentions

Every cell in my body was afraid when I heard Kalt's voice. I couldn't hear anything more after that. I couldn't even think of a proper cohesive thought, either. Before the world around me started to change, I did know that my father stood up from his seat. He glared at Kalt and started to speak. I couldn't hear a word of it. Only buzzing of sounds began to fill the room, and my vision of my father changed.

I felt small, looking up at my father, who now looked large. My seat was more prominent than a moment ago, and my dress was gone. I now had a coat of red fur, four paws, and a tail. I could only respond to my instinct of self-preservation. I rolled myself up in a ball and felt a hand carefully pick up my body. The hand I learned was my sister Julia's. She put me in her purse. It wasn't comfortable. However, it felt similar to a cave. All I could do was watch and wait. The hand Julia used to pick me up rested beside me. Despite her perfume, she had a smell that was familiar to my fur. She smelled like a wolf. There were moments when the buzzing sound got loud, and the buzzing stopped. It felt like a long time has passed since I found myself resting in that cave-like space. I slept only to be woken by occasional loud buzzing and banging sounds. When I woke, my instinct was to cuddle close to Julia's hand, which felt safe. She scratches my back and ears for a moment. Then her hand would rest on my back.

Suddenly I feel Julia's hand move in a different way than before. She picked me up again and pulled me out of the cave. I was carried in her hand while she moved her purse and placed it on her shoulder. She stood up and held me close to her chess. I felt a lot of eyes on me. A new hand was held out in front of me. It looked like a man's hand. I gave that new hand a sniff. It had a scent of a wolf. It was dad's hand. I crawled over to that hand. He held me close to him.

The next thing I saw was Cronos and his family coming to talk with us. I still couldn't understand what they were saying. It still sounds like a buzzing noise to me. I don't like it. A new hand came close to me. My body got tense since I didn't know whose hand it was. I moved so that I could fight back the threat. Father's free hand stopped the hand that was coming my way. I hear more buzzing sounds. Then dad started walking away from the group.

When dad stopped to take a seat, I noticed we were outside. It looks like a well-cared-for garden. Father set me down in the empty space beside him on a stone bench and sighed in a way that almost sounded like a low growl. He wiped his face with his hand and looked lost in thought. I find myself rolling over to get a better view of my father. Because of that, I had my belly exposed. I had a feeling that I really shouldn't. It's dangerous, this feeling told me. I rolled again toward my father's direction. I hear him laugh.

'Good, he is happy,' I thought to myself. It was the first thought I had in a while.

"Watching you play makes me happy," my father says.

I'm sorry if I caused you any trouble. I didn't mean or even plan to become a wolf. I felt like I couldn't think at all. I can't imagine what thoughts could have been said without my knowing.

Dad put his hand on my back.

"What happened is normal, given what you've been through. It does remind me that you're indeed my daughter, closer to me in blood than your sisters. Trust me, my dear Roxanne, I would've transformed into a wolf if you hadn't. I can't afford to turn feral like you had since I'm council leader. A leader can't lose their sense of self," he said.

Dad continued to explain, "As for your worries over your telekinesis not having a filter, don't worry. A feral mind cannot share a thought. The mind cannot think of reasoning when it's focused on surviving. The mind and body can only react to the world presented. After all, I don't think you would've wanted to intentionally hurt Cronos when he tried to pet you."

Then that strange hand was Cronos.

"I stopped him since I could see you were uncomfortable. I explained to him that you weren't in a good place to think clearly. You're a wolf, and you feel safe around your kin. Julia,

Amelia, August, and I are the only ones who can be close to you when you're feral. Although I predict that when Cronos has their own cubs, the cubs will let both parents hold them," father said.

I feel sad. I don't want to hurt anyone, especially Cronos. I like Cronos and want them to feel safe with our family.

"My thoughts exactly," dad said.

"If you feel safe enough. I'd like to talk with you in your human form. I think you'll need to understand what happened during the meeting since you turned feral," father requested.

I took my time changing back. It feels like a long time since I last tried to transform. I think I got my hairstyle messed up again. Only I don't care how my hair looks. It's longer than it had ever been since I was a child. That was what I was feeling now, like a little child.

"There's the young lady I know and love," father said with a smile.

His eyes seemed to smile with him as he moved some hair out of my face.

"I will start with the relatively good news first. The council agreed that you're too young to get married. Your feral form had helped in presenting a fair case. Your animal transformation showed the council your vampire blood is young. For most vampires who look as old as you do now, your form would be more mature and capable of defending your family. Among his other arguments, Kalt's case was that you look mature. The other arguments were the same as before with human age and laws," father started to recount and went silent for a spell.

He seemed lost in thought or perhaps trying to choose his following words carefully.

"That's good news, though. Even the council can now see that Kalt is out of line with this," I said, trying to assure my father.

"On one hand, yes, but on the other hand, no. This doesn't change anything for now. This will make life harder for you as you get older," father said with a tone of frustration.

"I don't get it. How is this going to make life harder for me?" I asked.

"If the time comes when you can have a relationship with a partner of your own, no vampire from this council will consider you," father started.

"Even though Kalt's action seemed foolish, he created a situation where you'll never be able to marry another vampire unless it was with him. He made it clear to everyone in that room today that they'll be his enemy if they consider looking at you with romantic intentions," he continued.

"I understand. To be honest with you, I'm not interested in having a relationship like that. I never felt that way as a human, and I still don't feel that way now. So even if that's the case, I'm okay being alone now. I am and will always be my own person if things change," I explained.

Father made a sound between a laugh and a sigh.

"I know you'll be fine when it comes to being on your own, my child. You're like me that way. Content as an alone wolf. You do have a strong character. However, I'm worried about any soul that truly loves you. Kalt will go after them. Kalt will deal with them whether you love them back or not," father replied.

"Wouldn't the council get involved if Kalt started going after people?" I asked.

"Only if it involved another council leader or future council leader. A simple clan member missing would never be reported to the council. Such cases are left to the clan's own heads to investigate. If it involves another clan, the deal between the two clans must be worked out for an investigation and disciplinary actions to occur. The council would hear about their death only if they're dead, and as you saw today, we don't request cause-of-death reports. Only affirmation of their deaths. Hence, after today, the clan leaders will tell their members to avoid you for their safety," father said.

"I see," I replied.

We sat in silence. I enjoyed the occasional breeze that passed by us. It felt like a hug from some unseen force. Even if it's not a romantic relationship, even if I tried to make friends with others, they could get hurt because of this. I would live alone if I didn't have my vampire family.

"Kalt will not hurt his kin, at least," dad said to break the silence and offer his peace in the mix of things.

Father continued, "He's foolish and reckless, but he'll toe the line with family. After all, it's in his best interest to foster some good well with us after this mess."

"Since he hadn't stopped after the courting stone mess and everything today, I want to believe you. I can't see any of his boundaries right now," I said.

"I know, but I promise that he has some. Sadly, this isn't out of character for him. Only when he hits the wall of how far he can take something will he step back or down from his desires," father said with a hand on my head and continued. "For now, we'll keep an eye out tentatively and look forward to good things one day at a time. I think it's time to head in. I need to talk with some people. I'd feel better if you stayed by my side for now. I'm sure that some council members would also like to meet you formally since your blood woke."

I did as dad asked. I met people and passively listened to conversations about politics. I hated the subject in school and cared for it less, given everything that happened. Yet I placed a smile on my face and kind, thoughtful words on my tongue. I can't let it show that Kalt has been getting to me. Speak of the devil. His mother is coming over to talk now. What's her name again? My father told me when he explained their history and problem with our family. Her name was.... Penelope Van Schlager. Dad's first wife was called Lina Van Schlager. Lady Van Schlager only spoke briefly to my father to apologize for her son.

Despite being beside my dad, she didn't look in my direction or acknowledge my presents. I understand that there's a conflict between them. Still, this situation involves me as well. Shouldn't I get an apology? At least some acknowledgment? .... I should let it go. That lady's presents stress me out as much as her son. I looked around but couldn't find a trace of him. I wonder if his mother told him to leave while my dad talked to other council members. I honestly can't even guess what's happening around me anymore. People are complicated, and this world feels even more complicated to me. How am I supposed to thrive in a world like this? It feels like everyone with power has a mask and agenda to save their hides.

August showed up by making her way through the crowd. She stood beside dad and me. I guess she had to talk with people while dad was taking care of me outside.

'Feeling better?' she asked telepathically while moving some hair out of my face.

I nodded and smiled. August could tell I wasn't being authentic in my response but seemed to let the matter be for now.

'We can talk about it some more when we have some free time,' August said again through telepathy.

After some time greeting and talking with people, August, dad, and I returned to our rooms. We saw Julia and Cronos playing blackjack with a deck of cards in the hallway. I wonder if they're waiting for us. They put up the game when they saw us coming. Cronos offered me a hug.

"Sorry I almost hurt you," I said.

"What are you talking about?" Cronos asked.

Then seeming to recall past events, Cronos continued, "O', you mean when your father stopped me from petting you? Roxanne, that would've been entirely on me. I was the one who tried to do something stupid. You just wanted to feel safe. I get it. No need for apologies. Anyway, you're back to being your real self now, and I've got an idea of how to find some fun."

"What are you planning?" August asked.

"I happen to know our little Roxanne likes music. How

about we create our own fun game involving music?" Cronos suggested.

"I appreciate your willingness to help me cheer up, Cronos. I'm not really in the mood to play games right now. I would like some quiet time to rest and destress right now if that's alright," I said, feeling bad for turning down the offer.

"Perhaps we can play a fun game next time. I heard you'll be staying with us soon," I suggested.

"That's true. I'll be moving in with you all in a few days," Cronos said reassuringly, "And I'll be bringing a friend with me when I come to visit you."

Father looked at Cronos. I could understand it was a concealed surprised look. This must be news to him.

"I know that this is a last-minute change of plans, sir. It's my father's and older brother's decision. They wanted to talk to you about it in private today. They don't wish to create any further surprises for tomorrow's business meeting," Cronos said, looking uncomfortable.

Likely this wasn't how Cronos had initially planned to give dad the message. My father thanked Cronos for letting him know, and he gave me the keys to our room as he left to meet the Strum family. Julia noticed my hair and asked me if I'd like a haircut. I thanked her and told her to wait until we were back home. I explained how I'd use my wolf form while going to bed tonight and would likely need another haircut later. She understood and gave me a hug. With my stress, I could transform into my feral-minded beast at any moment. It'd be a pain for Julia to cut my hair whenever I lose control.

"If you're going to get a haircut later, anyway," Cronos

started, "Can I hold you in your wolf cub form now that you're not feral?"

I smiled and said, "I don't mind. Fair warning though I can't control my telekinesis. I could end up thinking some weird stuff."

"Well, then you'll have some good company, little gem," Cronos said with a smile, "Wolf cub, please?"

I sighed and gave myself some time to change. The minute I finished my transformation, I felt hands scoop me up and press me close and tightly to their chess.

I thought to myself, Cronos, you're squishing me! Tight! To tight! Air! Air!

"Sorry! I didn't mean to hurt you, my little sis-gem. You're just so cute! A sweet little ball of fluff you are. It's hard to believe that one day you'll look like a majestic wolf," Cronos said apologetically.

Julia showed Cronos how best to hold me as a cub. They relaxed their hold and gently petted my back. I appreciate the changed position and felt comfortable. It would make sense that Cronos might need to know how to hold a wolf cub if their children inherit Julia's family skills.

"I was thinking the same thing," Julia said.

Cronos teased, "Guess that makes you the guinea pig in this family training practice, Roxanne."

I don't mind. With Julia as your teacher, I can breathe now. I'll give you a passing grade.

Cronos, Julia, and August giggle.

"Thank you, Roxanne," Cronos said.

"Should we put you to bed so you can rest, Roxanne?" August asked.

Yes, please, I thought while my cub's body yawned.

Julia opened the bedroom door with dad's key that I had put down on the floor before transforming. While Cronos carried me into the room, they placed me on the bed. August created a ring of pillows around me. That way, I'd feel like I was being cuddled.

"It helps young cubs feel safe. Seems like a smart thing to do given everything," August explained.

The bed feels cold, and the pillows do too. Yet I can get over my discomfort. I know that my body heat will warm the bed soon.

"That and your father will be back soon. I can't imagine that my father will keep him long," Cronos said.

"Would you like us to wait with you?" Julia asked.

Nope, I trust Cronos. I think that our father will be back soon. I also think that you'll want some time to catch up. It'd be boring to watch a cub sleep.

"O', I don't think that would be a problem for us. Especially since you're such a cute cub. Nevertheless, we'll let you sleep. If you need us, we'll be just outside the door until your father returns," Cronos said.

I thanked them. Julia turned the lights off, and all three of them headed out. I try to sleep. It felt like it took hours for sleep to find me. Then I hear the door quietly open and close. I didn't think much of it since it was likely dad. Then I feel ice-cold hands pick me up from the bed. I try to open my eyes to see, yet I can't. I try to move my body and squirm out of the person's hands, only I can't move. I felt paralyzed, but it wasn't out of fear. I was held close to a person's chest. This person was wearing a cold silk-like cloth.

Could this be a type of snare illusion? I'm in the form of an animal. Still, it can't be. Has anyone ever tried to snare a vampire with a snare illusion before? Can it work that way?

"You really do need to learn to control your telekinesis, cousin. There's no need to worry. I placed a communication filter around the room. No one can hear your thoughts or my words," Kalt said.

'Though I'll be talking with you from this point on with my own telekinesis,' Kalt explained by thought.

Why are you here? Haven't you done enough for one day?

'I'm here to help you. I know that there are blind spots that your family cannot see about this situation. I'll help fill you in. I know my behavior seems odd, but everything I've done is for your safety. Right now, what will keep you safe is if I presented myself toward you the same way my mother's been towards your father; infatuated. The fact is I hate you. Yet someone I hate more wants you dead. That means I need to take care of you,' Kalt thought.

I feel so confused and uncomfortable. Given everything I've learned these past nine days, I don't trust him.

'Then let's start from the beginning,' Kalt suggested.

'What do you know about my family and your father's relationships?' he inquired thoughtfully.

Well, I know your family hasn't shown preferable respect to my family since August came out as transgender. As evidenced by the first two nights, my blood woke. You picked a fight with her by using the wrong pronouns and nicknames. And...

'I'm asking what you know about your father's history with my Aunt Lina and my mother,' Kalt's intrusive thoughts interrupted.

Why not bring up your own history with my family and me if you want to know why I don't trust you?

'Trusting me or not is work you'll just have to sort out on your own. I'm trying to explain my behavior, and it starts by understanding theirs,' Kalt thought angrily.

Man, you're a controlling asshole.

'That's bold coming from a paralyzed cub,' he thought darkly.

Fine, I know that your mother has a thing for my father. When your Aunt Lina died from the plague, your mother tried to present that your father also died from the same thing. She tried to appeal to the council to let her and my dad get together. When she was rejected, she felt scorned by my father. Does that sum it up?

'Only part of it. Do you know how your father felt towards both my aunts? Why did he take so long to get married to either woman? Your mother wasn't old by our standards of living, but she was starting to get old by human standards when she had you,' Kalt reflected.

I don't know. I'd say that he had to love them on some level. Since he loves his children and he never spoke ill about them. Only that my mother went to places she shouldn't have been. Possibly showed off her talents and strengths too soon.

I still think it's out of genuine concern and love he has for her that he thinks that way about her.

'Then it's safe to assume that he hasn't told you that both marriages were arranged to meet the council's needs. His emotion towards people is the same as yours. He doesn't have a romantic bone in his body. Yet he'll build relationships and emotionally invest with people close to him, like family. Feelings like love take time for him to develop, if ever. The same can be said about you from what your friends have told me,' Kalt thought with no restraint.

There was an awkward pause.

'I'll tell you, my grandfather always planned for my mother to be a council leader. Before we were born, the council wasn't as diverse as it is now. Instead, there were separate councils consisting of only one type of vampire, except the infected. Our types had to intervene to prevent them from becoming monsters, which often happened in the early days. The idea of having all three in one space and governed was unthinkable. When my mother learned that the council would experiment with a possible merger between blood and sound eaters through a test by marriage, she requested to marry your father. My grandfather was against it. There were rumors about the sound council's strange new council member. That your father was a ruthless killer.

Grandfather didn't want the sound vampires to have any place in our polity. His opinion held much sway over the general council during that time. My mother was denied by our council. He didn't want to risk losing his future successor to a murderer. Instead, my grandfather knew precisely how uncomfortable he could make the situation be for his daughters. He wanted them to feel like victims of changing and unpredictable times. By doing so, he would make himself the hero. If they arranged for his youngest daughter, Lina, to be offered by our council to become your father's wife. Many hoped it would fail because it was arranged. They bet and never could imagine sweet Lina would ever upset her beloved older sister. They also hoped that your father's rumored violent nature would provide justification for why they couldn't change. Especially being offered the most pleasant of the blood councils women for a wife. A sure failure plan to screw your father over. Your father first denied wanting to marry Aunt Lina. He only accepted my aunt's hand in marriage after learning it was a test. Only to prove the blood council wrong and that a possible merger could happen. That their marriage could be a happy one. It probably took time for them to learn to love each other and their daughters.

Seeing them happy made my mother resentful and sick since neither initially loved the other. She hates the council and its rules. She hated her father, too. The final straw that broke the camel's back was when your mother entered the picture. That marriage was also arranged by the council but for a different reason.

Twenty-five years ago, our collective council didn't know what to do about valuable humans like your mother. Often such people who had rare gifts were protected by vampire hunters. They did a good job keeping them away from any of our kind. Aunt Aria didn't have a protector and needed protection. She used to be all over the place and easy prey. Your father was arranged to be her protector as the oldest member. He'd be the wisest to guide her wild and naive nature. Seven years after starting his work as her protector, the council felt that the role of protector wasn't enough for the situation. They requested that your father and mother get married. Even though I don't understand their reasoning to this day, marriage was considered the safest choice for her. That's why she became his second wife. Do you remember anything about the day your mother died, Voxy?' Kalt reflected and pondered.

I try to think back about any memories I've had with my mother. I only remember the one with the patio swing and sunset. A shadow moving in the tree that I'm not even sure really happened.

'So, you only remember that moment. I also remember that day. It was the day before your mother died. I was the shadow in the tree, as you put it. My mother was truly sick then. Not only did she want your mother dead, but she ordered me to kill you. No one else should have the privilege she used to tell me. As a pure-blooded vampire, it's my responsibility to kill mistakes like you out of mercy. I couldn't return home until I handed your corpse to her. That day was painful trying to hide from the sun. I don't know if I should've been as grateful as I was. I was spotted by the child I was supposed to kill. You gave me an excuse to return home when you found me in the tree that day and told your mother. With you knowing I was there, it'd only be a matter of time before your father would also know. My mother would've had a trail connecting her to the death of your mother and you. She couldn't hide evidence of events with the risk. We were positive that your father taught her how to hide secret messages for him to find out if something should happen to either one of you. I was severely punished for getting caught by you. It was a reprieve from the number of days I had to survive being close to sunlight. Awake when I should've been sleeping,' he thought with an ice-like glaze in his eyes.

Did your mother kill her then? What does any of that have to do with what is happening now?

'Are you trusting my word again? If you want the truth, find the truth. I'm not going to do all the work for you. I'll warn you that I will be a pain in your ass until my mother dies. That means I'll have to be a bad guy. But you're used to it by now. I've been actively intervening in my mother's schemes against you,' he thought dismissively.

I felt my anger building up from Kalt's thoughts.

'Do you want to know why Bruce had that job for as long as he did and wasn't sent packing after sleeping with his first female customer? It's because she hired him, not me. There is a protection policy at the club where I can't fire any of my mother's employees, and she can't fire any of mine. The only exception to that policy between my mother and me is if cultural legal charges against an employee require them to be fired due to misconduct. Your friend with the green hair, bless her heart, provided reasonable cause for an investigation for me to get him a pink slip out of the club. I couldn't fire him until there was a formal complaint about his behavior. My mother did a good job keeping the women quiet. She altered their memories of the encounters. Just long enough to ensure you'd show up for your eighteenth birthday. I kept you from that drink. I kept you away from her employees. With what my mother had planned for you, your birthday would've been the day you would regret being alive. Bruce wasn't our only concern that night. But you're a smart girl and could probably tell there were traps set for you that night. Uncle will be here soon; I need to go. This will be the last time I can talk with you like this, cousin,' Kalt remembered and reflected coldly.

With that, Kalt put me down in a nest of pillows on the bed and left the room. It felt like a moment had passed after Kalt left and when I heard the door open again. I heard dad sigh, and the bed moved. I think he just plopped himself on the bed next to me. I open my eyes to see him looking up at the ceiling. Father must've heard the plop thought yet seems unresponsive. I know my telekinesis still has no filter, so he can hear that thought.

"Yes, I can hear you, my dear Roxanne. I thought you were trying to sleep, my child. We both have had an eventful day," father groaned.

"I'm sorry for my mood right now, child. Dealing with the council is draining. In the past, I had some energy left after all these meetings. I used to be able to spend time with your sisters afterward. However, I'm spent today. I'll turn into a wolf soon. But first, a quick rest," father said with a yawn.

2

The Bloody Immortal

I couldn't go back to sleep. I ended up watching dad rest and attempt to climb on top of his chest. Father chuckled when I slid off after getting so close. He helped me up on his chest.

"Child, I love you. Watching you and your sisters grow is the greatest joy in my life," father groggily said.

I felt sick with guilt. I believe dad. I love him and my sisters so much. However, it isn't easy for me to love people outside my family. Is that a bad thing? I wonder.

"What makes you think that, my dear?" my dad asked.

I'm just thinking about how odd I can seem to others. Even as a human, I wasn't interested in falling in love like my peers. I was content with just having friends. With how things have been lately.... I gave a squeaky-sounding growl. Father, I need to tell you something. You asked me to be honest with you about what I'm learning. Before you got here, Kalt was here to talk. I feel my head hurt remembering Kalt's visit.

"What did Kalt want to talk about?" father enquired, trying to withhold his anger.

He said that he wanted to help protect me from his mother. He asked me what I knew about your relationship with his mother and your first wife, Lina. He thinks it affected his mother's relationship with my mother and me. He asked if I remembered what had happened when my mother died. He told me what the council used to be like. That your marriages were arranged by the council. He also told me that my only memory with mom was the day before she died. That the shadow I remember moving in the tree that day was him. I don't remember telling my mother about it. Kalt did, though. He said he was punished by his mother for getting caught, as I try to recall the visit.

I watched my dad's eyes get glassy. He seemed to be lost in thought or perhaps lost in memories.

If it helps, Kalt assured me that he's not interested in a relationship with me. It's an act to keep his mother away from me until his mother dies, I reminisced.

Father sighs and holds his head.

"There is much wrong with that child's assumptions. For starters, a vampire will never know when another vampire will die. The only exception to that rule that we know of concerns the infected. We've learned that no matter how healthy they live, they'll die after a hundred years. Lady Van Schlager may outlive her own son. Using his mother's history as an excuse for his behavior doesn't give him an out.

Secondly, even if he tells himself it's an act, he is practicing a behavior that he won't easily be able to unlearn. It also doesn't take away from the reality that his behavior has affected the lives of others. His behavior has created anxiety for you and will limit what you can look forward to. Things that other people can have freely. For example, you got tense on our way to today's council meeting.

Furthermore, you were so scared during today's meeting you turned feral-minded and transformed into a wolf because of what he did. As I said earlier, I would have turned into a wolf if I could. His behavior is affecting me too. I'm sure the same can be said for your sisters," father vented.

Then father grabbed a pillow from my nesting spot and groaned into it. After a moment of silence, he tossed the pillow off the bed.

"I need to tell you everything about me. It's not like I ever planned to keep it a secret from you or the rest of my children. I'd rather you all didn't know if none of you thought to ask. It's time to come clean, at least to you, Roxanne. Remember how I told you that our vampire history isn't pretty?" he asked.

Dad put me back into the nest of remaining pillows while setting up on the bed. I nodded. I couldn't forget that book even if I wanted.

"Your sisters know I'm old. Except they don't know this. I'm one of the first humans who was changed into a vampire. In a sense, I was turned but not infected. We have a word for a vampire like me who's not born a vampire yet is full-blooded. Vampires like me who've gone through this type of change live much longer than all vampires. This is why vampires like me are called immortals. The truth is that even an old vampire like me can still die. I just haven't died yet. Many immortals consider each other brothers and sisters. Only because there are few of us. Over the years, the number of immortals grows less as some have died. I know because some of my brother and sister immortals have been killed by my hand.

There were once five hundred eighty-nine immortal natives in this land before the colonization. Today there are only three native immortals. Two blood-eating immortals and one sound-eating immortal. Five immortals immigrated here, counting myself. All of us were sent due to councils' overseas orders. The last international census on vampires reports that immortals comprise 0.000012% of our population.

The only type that doesn't have any immortals is infected. We think that at one time, there were infected immortals. However, it could be that they simply couldn't live a longer life beyond some point in time. Similar to how their turned kin can only live 100 years. Care to guess how old I am, my dear child?" father tested.

I'd say as old as Jesus. However, Julia, Cronos, and Kalt are 2000 years old and were born around that time. I would assume that you're older than that. You wouldn't happen to be old enough to have lived during the time of the dinosaurs, would you? I jokingly pondered.

"Depends on the type of dinosaurs," father said with a smile.

He didn't sound like he was joking back. Is he serious?

"I'm very serious. I am 52,582 years old, to be exact.

After a few centuries, years mean little to nothing. Trust me, I'm not the oldest nor youngest of the immortals left in our world. However, I'm one of the many first humans when I was human," dad continued to answer.

That would mean you had your first vampire child when you were a few years over fifty thousand. When did you get married to Lina? How soon were you able to have children? Did you have any children when you were human?

Dad sighs and says, "I'll get to that. Let's start with the beginning. That way, you can have a chance to hear everything in order. Plus, I don't have to worry about missing anything you should know. That last thing I want is for you to feel like I'm keeping something important from you."

With that, father explained, "As you can imagine, over 52,000 years ago, our world was much different. We had no laws. We had no countries. We were humans, but we weren't a people. The law that governed humankind was the same as nature itself.

People may fantasize about how wonderful living in a 'simple time' would be. I wouldn't change our world back to that time for anything. Only the fit and favored survived in the world. It was a bloody and violent place to live. Indeed the peak of inhumanity itself.

I lived in the moment like many humans at the time. We lived to survive. We did what felt good, whether it helped or hurt others. I could've been a few human children's father, but I never knew. There was no such thing as a structured family, as we understand families today. Males would never stay with a female. Nor did a parent stay with their child. I couldn't even tell you what your grandmother was like. I have no memories of her.

We did what was easy, which often meant stealing and killing. I killed animals of all kinds. I killed more than animals, too. This is where my dark past comes to light. I also killed more humans than I can count. I killed humans who got in my way. I killed those who tried to steal what I had. I killed people to take what they had. Sadly, I also killed some just because I was able and bored. From adults to children, there was no exception to whom I killed back then. It wasn't hard for someone like me to do enough beastly acts to become a vampire. Though, it's not like I could know such actions would lead to a cursed life.

One strange day, a group of men spotted me while I was hunting a sabretooth tiger. After I killed the beast, they tried to kill me for my hunt. Being attacked over food was ordinary. What wasn't normal at that time was that they were a group. Most humans don't hunt in packs. Even if they dwell together, they tend to hunt individually. They cut up and broke my right arm because of their combined strength. They broke three ribs and cracked my skull. The injury caused me to lose a small part of my skull bone on the upper left side. I still have that small hole there today. New skin and muscle have grown over that old wound. I also had a punctured lung. You'll see my old scars when I'm in my wolf form tonight.

Honestly, I rarely turn into a wolf these days. When your sisters were younger, they saw my form while learning to become wolfs. Perhaps they thought it was normal for an old wolf to have scars. They never ask me about it. My daughters only excepted my old scars as a part of me. Shall I show you what I look like now?"

I nodded. Watching my father closely.

"Very well," dad said.

He started his transformation into a wolf. It was different from August's wolf form. His fur was longer and thicker. He looked more muscular and taller than August's wolf. His claws also looked thicker and sharper. His red coat had patches that were a darker shade of red. The place where dad said he had his head injury was one of those darker red spots. He climbed on the bed and curled next to my cub form. Despite the rough look of his fur, it's soft and warm. His coat smelled of metal and wolf hormones.

'My child, with how science finds new facts every day, I could be something else than an old wolf. Calling this form a wolf makes it easier. Some wanted to call me a dire wolf in the past. I would let them. I don't think we will ever know what this form actually is until the end of time,' father explained through telekinesis.

You look fantastic even with those old injuries; I couldn't help thinking.

'Well, I was stubborn. I had no intention of going down without a fight. I fought back and killed fourteen of the fifteen people. I didn't realize I was changing. I believed I was slowly dying at that time. I watched the fifteenth person flee. I lost all thought. Then I went feral. My feral form was this. Like yours was this morning. With my body changed, I caught the last person and tortured them. They died a slow and painful death. I felt myself becoming more robust and renewed every time they screamed in pain.

I kept wondering after that man died. I expected death. However, death didn't come. I kept living. Life felt strange to me. When I became a vampire, I had a new hunger.

I wandered the world for forty thousand years. I ate living sound energy from nature and humans alike. I killed nearly every person I met. I saw civilizations form, change, and fall. Towns became the best feeding grounds. It's as convenient as a bear finding a beehive. I was naturally hunted as a threat to villages and cities alike. Over that time, my hair became red to the root from the blood of my victims.

Some humans tried to seek aid from me in times of war. I betray them all in the end. I always had the upper hand. It didn't matter how they protected themselves from me. It was rare when I came across another vampire. Some were immortals like me. Many were full-blooded or half-blooded. I came out on top of our bloody fights except one.'

Father stopped and licked my head.

He continued reminiscing, 'I'm glad I lost to the vampire I did. If not for him, I wouldn't have you or your sisters. I wouldn't know how to control my abilities or hunger. I wouldn't have seen how different this world became while stuck in the past. Though humans seemed all the same to me, vampires were changing. They considered how they could learn to relate to the world differently than merely hunting and living. They were learning along with humanity.

I met this fellow sound vampire in the country of Turkey. His name was Emir Berat. He was a born full-blooded vampire, like your sisters. He met other sound vampires who were feral-minded and adopted them into his clan. Vampires needed to trust others and build relationships to be adopted into a clan.

I fought Emir while he was traveling with his clan to a council meeting. He protected his family from me when I ambushed their camp. He wasn't as physically strong as I was. We were equal in creating strategies and plans during the fight. However, Emir understood how to use living energy in ways I didn't. In the end, that knowledge prevented me from landing a hit. He never attacked back. He only defended himself and others. Emir won by letting me use up my energy. I expected a final blow to kill me, but it never came. He simply asked me if I was done fighting with him. That cheeky so-so.

Seeing that I couldn't fight back, Emir told me he hadn't met a feral vampire like me. I gave him quite the time, and he wanted to know why. I had no interest in answering his questions and stayed silent. They ended up bringing me with them to their council. It took days for me to learn to trust Emir enough to talk.

When I spoke with Emir, he told me I'd be considered an immortal. He told me that even at that time, old immortals were becoming few to find. He was glad to meet one as rare as me. He explained that new immortals were born almost every day. The reason for this was wars and extreme civil oppression.

He illuminated many things to me. He explained how he beat me in our fight despite my strength. Where he and his kin were going. What having a family and clan is like? He shared how things have changed from stories he learned from his father and grandfather.

When we arrived at the house for the council meeting, Emir asked me if I'd like to be adopted into his family's clan. I agreed. He inquired if we had names for ourselves in the past. I told him technically, we didn't. Others called me Gra briefly before I was given other names. I didn't think they're intended as a personal name.'

I squeaked with laughter as a cub.

Gra, that was your name?

'Is that funny to you, my dear cub? Perhaps I should've given you a different name. Since you think it's so amusing, father pondered.

That got me to stop squeaking.

I'm good. Sorry for upsetting you, father. I'll listen.

Dad looked at me as if to say are you sure?

Then father continued to share his story.

'Over time, I had been called pest, beast, abomination, and monster. Emir felt I needed a new name. I was told I needed a real name to be officially presented to his council. He named me Kirmizi Van Kurt after seeing my bloody red wolf form. I didn't know that my friend Emir was planning for something more than adoption.

During that meeting, he named me as his future successor to his family's clan. Many in his clan naturally objected to the move. Later I learned that those who opposed were Emir's children and grandchildren. They were expecting to be the next clan's successor. Emir had nineteen wives and many children. Their children had many children, too. Even today, his grandchildren, great-grandchildren, and great-great-grandchildren are opposed to my authority.

When I asked Emir why, he told me his kin were losing strength and power. They've seen it with each generation. Children are becoming less powerful than their parents. He feared that no one would be capable of protecting his clan if he died. Emir said if he died in our fight, none of his children could hold their own against me. He told me that whether his family liked it or not, the night I came into their lives was a gift. I've more experience in a fight than they had. I wasn't troubled by the sight of death like they were. He told me that I could learn even though I wasn't educated or used to relationships.

Since then, I learned much about culture, taboos, monsters, politics, economics, ethics, and how to write and read many languages. Emir also taught me how to use living energy beyond my natural transformation into a wolf. In return, I taught him what I'd learned and seen over the years. I helped reinforce Emir's rules when his clan members got out of hand. Life was complicated those five thousand years before Emir died. I started getting used to my role, and some of the clan got used to me.

At times, Emir had to leave to exterminate the monsters that showed themselves. The very same monsters in that one book you read your first day. One summer day before a council meeting, a man who left to fight a monster with Emir returned. This man told me Emir had died. I became the clan's leader out of the blue.

At that council meeting, I shared the news of Emir's death

and had the witness testify about the events. The council acknowledged me as the new leader of the Berat clan. The council decided another clan would be responsible for slaying the monster that killed Emir. I wanted to protest, but they wouldn't let me. I was new and had no successor to take my place. If I was sent to finish what Emir started and meet the same fate, Berat's clan would be in chaos.

Those who didn't care for me tested me during my leadership's first two hundred years. During that time, conflicts with other vampires' councils were popping up in neighboring countries. Clans knew Emir were being moved out to help other councils to share information and provide peace. While new clans from different regions came to our council to learn from our experience.

Eventually, I was assigned to move with my clan to Germany. I was supposed to help support a sound council there. When I arrived, I was told the sound council wanted to make peace with a neighboring blood council. There had been blood vampires hunting sound vampires for years over land. They couldn't simply work together because the blood council was very strongly divided. They couldn't agree on what they wanted in a governing body. As a result, communication problems in the whole blood council prevent them from making peace. That was the information I was told, but the real problem was something else.

After our first meeting between the two councils, it was apparent that the blood council had an internal power hierarchy. This met that some leaders had more power over other leaders. They manipulate and passively change its laws to give some people with power more say than others. Those seeking to create equality in power often were met with isolation by those who had power. Since sound councils practice equal social and governing standing among leaders, it was understandable that they would've problems. Those with power in the blood council wouldn't see the sound council as equals. Only invaders trying to break them. The ability to navigate and adapt political practice with a different approach was beyond either group. Both councils had people who wanted things to change. Many, even those with opposing power, wanted a sign to decide what change should come. Those with power in the blood council want any indication of unity to fail. I met many human governing bodies like the blood council. However, I have had the luxury of never needing to truly get involved.

The sound council I was assigned wasn't any better, to be honest. The sound council needed to change their relationships with the blood council. Except they refused to risk taking any actions out of fear of possible war over any enforced compromise. That's why they chose me to be in the conversation for them with the blood council. If things worked out, they could reap the benefits of avoiding a war breaking out over territories. If something went south, they could tell other sound councils that they did try to make peace. Only a nosy outsider tried to ruin their attempt. That I was never really one of their sound clan council members since I only arrived.

It's only half true when Kalt said I declined to marry his aunt. By the third meeting, the blood council offered an opportunity for me to marry one of their ladies. I explained that

I needed to stay impartial. If I did agree to accept a marriage proposal, it would need to be approved by the sound council.

I had to inform the sound council of the blood council's offer for me to marry. They encouraged it. Later, I learned that this arrangement was to show how incompatible a relationship between types could be.

I never told the blood or sound councils that vampire power weakened over generations. I'm sure some clans could see the power difference. It's not freely shared knowledge. I confess that I was afraid of raising a child weaker than myself.

My fears were put to rest after meeting my arranged wife-to-be, Lina. In a short time, we found common ground very fast. It helped us break the ice that she was also uncomfortable with the arrangement. She felt comfortable enough to talk about her family's history with the sign of a bat. I told her it sounded like the same reason my family name is a wolf. She taught me about her family's transformation into a bat. She was elated to learn that I could transform into one. I was surprised, too. I did come to love her, and she liked me.

We found more income than either council wanted. The two had to meet and work together without proof of conflict in our marriage. You know, two thousand years and eleven months ago, we asked to have a child and were blessed with Julia. Then about seven hundred years after Julia was born, we had Amelia. Then August came about four hundred years after that. Life was challenging but promising. The merger was a true challenge with power struggles. People didn't want to let go of what power they had for who knows how long they had it. Once things appeared to be calm, we had neighboring councils come and observe our new practice.

Lina was a caring woman who was slow to anger and willing to compromise to meet the family's needs. She wanted us not to tell your sisters about our marriage being arranged. Lina didn't want her girls to fear that they would be political tools in life and marriage. She always told me she was glad I was chosen to be her husband. If Lina had a say in the matter, she would've liked it more if she had been the one to pick me instead. She didn't care for illusions, except telekinesis. Nor did she care for humor. Considering how much our daughters love to tease, joke, and play, I still find it interesting. She educated your sisters on how to use their vampire abilities.

The only thing I could teach them was how to eat since they're sound vampires and how to transform into wolfs. My dear poor Lina, I remember she tried one time to transform into a wolf but couldn't. She felt so ashamed that our daughters could do something she couldn't. You already know how she died.

I never thought it odd that she could get sick during that time. We were among people regularly because of our political work. I wonder if she could've contracted it because of her sister. If not her sister, then other vampires who felt disempowered because of the merger of councils. At the end of the day, I have many enemies just being myself and my position.

It wouldn't surprise me if your mother's death was planned. I don't know what happened to her because your mother died during the daylight. I could only spend time with you both during the night. I would care for you while your mother slept as an infant. It was the only time back when you were human that I could spend time with you. I bond with you as I had done for your sisters. I had even less time to be with you as you learned to sleep through the night. Despite visiting your mother's house every evening, I couldn't prevent what happened.

I was scared that day that I lost you both. I was thrilled to find you alive and sleeping in a clever place no one would've thought to look for you. I only found you after I transformed into a wolf. I can smell and know if an animal or person is my kin. I tracked you down. Don't ask about where I found you. I don't know for sure why you were there. I can only guess you might've been hiding from the person who killed your mother.

I called the human authority to inform them that someone found your mother dead. You were left alone in the house. Pretending to be a third-party person was the only way to explain why I couldn't be there. The minute I finished that call, I tried to get in contact with your mother's sister. We've never talked or met, making getting hold of her challenging. It's disturbing how long the human system took to turn you over to your aunt and uncle's care. That goes to show how complicated the human world is to me.'

My father stopped sharing his thought with me. He looked sad and uncomfortable, with his eyes closed and tail twitching more frequently. I licked my father's wolf cheek. He couldn't cry being a wolf. Though, I can imagine what he would look like if he was in his human form.

Thank you for telling me what you can, father. I know

you've also been through a lot these last few days. Heck, you've been through a lot in several lifetimes. I understand that the past is messy and dark. Thank you for being thoughtful and protecting us. I know you've always done your best to keep us safe. I have a better understanding of how you love our mothers and us.

'There is one more thing you should know before we sleep, my dear child. You truly are different than your sisters and any other vampire we know. We call you a half-blood because your mother was human, yet there is more to you. Over time your mother's blood will die off like every other half-blood vampire. You'll live out the rest of your life on my vampire blood.

Because you lived as a human for eighteen years, your body may have aged like other half-bloods. Although, the same can be said for me before I changed into a vampire, too. I'm positive that when the day comes that your mother's blood entirely dies out, you'll become an immortal vampire, too. The only immortal vampire born without experiencing inhumanity.

Historically, most immortals try to never mingle with humans. Often out of pain that changed them or believing they should only mix with other vampires. You're an exception to the rule of generations becoming weaker. If anything, you're a constant. You're equal to me in power. Sadly, you may also be similar to me in blood lust. This is why I'll do everything possible to prevent you from making another person bleed. I refuse to see that past revisited in your life.

People will hate you for being who you are. Never let that

stop you from living an honest life. Kalt's mother probably does hate us and may want you dead. Kalt may play his games with us for who knows how long. No matter what happens, live your own life well.

It's okay if it takes time to find love. It's also okay that you simply don't love the same way others do. I only ask that you'll use your power to protect your sisters and their families if something should ever happen to me. They have their own power and know how to use it well. However, I know you have all of mine and will have more time to learn how to use that power. Can I ask this of you, my dear Roxanne?' father wondered.

I will help them as I am able. I still don't know much about this world. I'm still learning much from all of you each day. I haven't mastered any illusions, I have no control over my telekinesis, and I still can't control my hair after a transformation. Hell, I don't even know who is a human and a vampire when I meet a random person on the street. I may have your power, but I doubt I could fight like you. I know I have good instincts, but if that's the case, why am I constantly finding out things I never knew about people I thought I knew? I can't help feeling if people trust me, it's misplaced. I felt lost as a human trying to figure out how to be an adult. I feel even more lost as a vampire. I can feel my mind continue to list every flaw in my person till dad's thoughts reach me.

'You are young. Only nine days old as a vampire. I'm sorry for putting so much pressure on you out of the blue, my daughter. I only ask this because I know someday, not now, you'll be able. I've no intention of dying anytime soon. That burden would never fall on your shoulders if I had it my way. But as immortal as I am, I know I can still die someday. I simply want to ensure that if it comes, all my children can and will thrive,' father nuzzled me with these assuring thoughts.

'As stressful as today was, tomorrow will come with its challenges. We can look forward to seeing Amelia, being home, and resting as a family after all this. Think of what makes you happy as you sleep, my dear child. For there will be better days ahead of us,' father continues to reflect with me.

With that, we went to sleep. Even in the cold house, I was warm, comfortable, and safe, cuddled close to my wolf-shaped father.

3

Fly on the Wall

Strange. Where am I? I find myself standing in a large field with patches of wildflowers. Around this vast field are tall trees like a forest. I walked around, trying to think if I had ever seen a place like this once before. I don't believe that I have seen any place like this in my life. No people. No bugs. No birds or rodents. How odd. I don't dream. What is this place? As I look around again, I see a child beside me. A girl, perhaps.

The child wore a black and white dress. The dress had fluffy white wool around the collar and sleeves. She also had black and white spiraled ram horns on her head. I wonder if the horns were painted. The child had a black and white umbrella in her right hand. Why? It was sunny in this place, and not a single cloud was in the sky. It is hard to describe what she looked like from that point on.

Her appearance kept changing. When I first saw her, her

hair was long and black. Then it was short curly blond. Now it is a carrot red, wavy, and mid-length. Her eyes are strange. Or should I say eye? Her right eye was solid white. While her left eye had an eye embedded inside. I really don't know how else to explain it. The inner eye was bloody red with a black pupil. The outer eye changed colors like their hair. I think I will be sick if I observe the constantly changing appearance. I had to turn my face away.

Then I hear the child say, "Sorry if I made you uncomfortable, Voxy Ann Van Kurt. Most people can't see me. I'm a leaf among trees in places such as this."

The child giggled.

"Where is this place? Who are you?" I ask.

"You're a person who doesn't dream. That's sad. I wanted to talk to you for a while. I couldn't contact you until now. For a person like me to speak to people like you, I had to learn to create a dream space. A dream space is created from living energy taken from other people's dreams. I suppose you can say I invited you to spend some time in my dream since you don't have your own.

As for who I am? I am myself. I'm not as strong as you. I'm the fifth child of my father's twenty-one wives. I have wanted to meet you since I learned about you and your family. I want to warn you about the present state of dreams. A danger will soon come in the wake of days," the child explained.

"You didn't really answer my question about who you are. You said that you used living energy to create dreams. Does that make you a vampire?" I ask.

The child said nothing. They only looked at me with wonder.

"You said that you have a warning for me. What is it?" I continue to ask.

The child smiled, and the dream faded.

I was in a dark empty space with my mind feeling fully awake. I didn't learn anything. Was that a real dream? Or am I starting to learn to dream? I doubt a person can learn to dream.

I ended up waking before my father. I think I should prepare for the day and let my father rest. However, I felt like waking him as a mischievous cub. I pounced on his tail to make it twitch. I climbed on his back. I pawed his nose. He started to wake up from my play. Father yawned and looked at me with sleepy eyes. He wasn't going to ask why I was waking him. He laid his head back down and watched me play. I did for a few minutes. I couldn't explain why I wanted to do this.

Could it be my cub's mind? Or is it something on an unconscious level? I wish I could've bonded with dad more as a child. I feel free to act like a child being a cub.

'I feel the same way, child. I wish that I could've bonded with you more when you were a child. I'll not stop you from playing because it brings me joy,' father shared his thought with me.

'Did you sleep well, my cub?' he inquired thoughtfully.

I guess. I have a question for you, though. Can vampires create dreams? I pondered while chasing my tail.

Father looked confused by the question.

'Yes, vampires can dream while sleeping. You told me

you don't dream but reflect on memories as you sleep. What brought this question? Did you have a dream last night?' father reflected.

Yes, you could say that. I considered that thought for a moment.

'Was it a bad dream, my dear cub?' father wondered.

It wasn't much of anything at first. Only a large field and a forest around it, as I reminisced.

'That sounds like a good dream. Sounds quiet and peaceful,' father thought.

I guess. It was just strange to me. I think I should turn back to myself to continue this conversation. I shared this thought with my father as I started to change back to my old self.

I hopped off the bed to transform back. Father yawned and stretched before he got out of bed, too. By the time I finished my transformation, dad was already back to being human. I know I'm slow in my transformation process. I'm afraid of messing it up. However, I can't help but wonder if I will someday be able to transform as fast as he can.

Anyway, I needed to figure out how to ask dad the right question. He clearly didn't understand what I meant. What would that space or ability be called? Is it an illusion? I don't think so. I would've seen it in the book if it was a known illusion ability. I doubt it's a transformation thing. Perhaps a manifestation ability? What makes a manifestation ability? I don't think it could be a manifested space. If it was a manifested space, wouldn't it have to be physical? Or possess properties of a physical space? Can something be manifested without existing? Then it would be an idea. Okay, I'm getting confused.

I feel dad watching me. He's already dressed for the day while I've thought deeply.

"Are you alright, my child?" he asked.

"You seem out of it this morning," father continued while placing a hand on my head.

"I'm trying to find the best way to explain my question. I think I poorly explained what I meant to ask you earlier," I replied.

"Is it possible for vampires to feed through dreams? How would you describe our ability to feed? Is it an illusion or manifestation?" I asked.

Father looked thoughtful for a moment.

Then he said, "To be honest with you, my Roxanne, I never thought about how we would define our method of eating. We cannot eat sound through dreams for a few reasons. First, we sleep when it's daytime when most humans are awake. The second reason would be that we would have to use much living energy to reach a sleeping mind. The return wouldn't be worth the energy invested. The only other option that could make sense is to sleep during the night like humans. Although, I don't think we could call ourselves living if we slept all day and all night. But that is only how I see it, child. For me, living means being able to wake up from sleep. As for the final reason, I don't think we can eat through sleep. I have never heard of a vampire who has ever tried. How I would describe how we feed; would be a beyond skill. A rare beyond skill since it's the only one common to every vampire. The matter of how is different depending on the type of vampire. We just consider it an ability to feed, nothing more."

I feel awkward asking my question to dad now. I wonder if dad has questions of his own after my odd questions. He probably wants to know what would make me even consider the idea of dream-eating. He doesn't ask. Nevertheless, I think I gave him something to consider. He looked lost in thought. Perhaps that person wasn't a vampire after all. If not a reckless vampire. Still, suppose they were a type of vampire. In that case, they choose to communicate through an ability closely related to feeding. Or perhaps they have a dream related beyond skill? At least it sounds similar to how sound vampires feed on living energy. That's scary. Does that mean they've been feeding on me since I was in their feeding space?

I dressed for the day, reflecting on all these thoughts and questions. I picked a white dress shirt and wore a gray sweater vest. I also brought an emerald green skirt with a lily print pattern. The hat Julia let me borrow seemed to go well with the look.

I asked dad when I was finished, "What will happen today?"

He hugged me and said, "I still have to finish council business today. August will be with me. You and Julia are free to find things to do while we finish. When we are done, we can go home and enjoy this day as a family. Perhaps we can finally teach you how to control your telekinesis."

We ate and met up with August and Julia, who were waiting for us in the hallway. August went with dad to the meeting. While I stayed with Julia in her room. She offered to cut my hair again, but I declined.

"A lot could still happen today. If it's alright with you, Julia, I'll wait until we get home. That way, we don't have to look forward to many more surprises," I said.

Julia looked concerned by my reluctance.

"I promise to let you cut my hair when we get home. Okay, Julia?" I say, trying to assure her.

Julia sighed.

"Alright. I'll hold you to this promise," Julia said.

We hear a knock on the door.

A familiar voice sings, "My love, My heart, will you please let me in? Your knight in shining armor is here to see you."

Julia blushed and chuckled as she went to open the door.

I laughed unapologetically.

When Cronos entered the room, they kissed Julia passionately. Until they realized I was in the room, too.

"I'm glad to see that your passion for my sister is still burning strong and bright," I said with a cat-like grin.

"Ah, the precious gem Roxanne is here. How has thou slept, dear sister of my eternal love?" Cronos enquired.

They walked over to the bed where I sat with a jar of something.

"I slept well, given yesterday's drama," I replied.

"How about you, Cronos? Dream sweet dreams of your future wife?" I asked.

"Always, my sister gem, always!" Cronos chimed.

"I must confess, some days I cannot sleep well. Heaven forbids a time I'm without thinking of my love every hour of every day. I morn the moment she leaves my thoughts," Cronos said, looking pitiful.

I laugh and say, "Truly, you're in love, Cronos."

"That I am, little gem, that I am," Cronos said, almost singing.

"Anyway, I thought we'd be tired of waiting for the meeting to finish today. And I know you're still learning the ways of a vampire, little gem. So I thought we could work on snare illusion to eavesdrop on the meeting. If able, we can irritate Kalt, too," Cronos proposed.

Cronos showed me the jar they were carrying. Inside the jar were three fruit flies.

"I thought because of a fly's complex vision, they're challenging to snare," I said.

"That is true. However, there is no easy way to learn snare than to simply try. We'll close the door and practice until we feel comfortable enough to let our flies roam outside," Cronos suggested.

Julia chimed, "August and I told Cronos about father's absence the last few days. They understand how challenging that time was for us. We agreed it might be time for us to learn how to use illusions with how things are going. Even though we never needed to use them for hunting. Illusions can be helpful for our protection and awareness. A fly or two will not require a lot of energy to snare, especially if Kalt puts us in a similar situation again."

I think I understand their point of view. It's better to have more skills than is needed for some situations. That is if the problem can be prepared for in advance. I agreed to learn how to snare a fly with them. I tried to remember the section of the illusion book that talked about the snare techniques.

The type of creature will determine the best way to put the beast in a snare trance. For most animals, making eye contact is the easiest way to snare. It's the easiest for a few reasons.

First, the eyes don't have the same sensitive nervous system as other organs. Since eyes adjust to different lights and with different pressures all the time without thought, it makes it easier to channel living energy without raising the alarm. Like many sensory organs, the eyes are closely related to sharing information with the mind. That makes snaring the host's mind quicker without time to raise a mental alarm to resist.

Despite the effectiveness of this method to snare, there are times and types of creatures it doesn't work well on. Cases that wouldn't work well would be creatures that are blinded, born without eyes, camouflaged, covered eyes, or sleeping. The reason again comes down to nerves and sensitivity. A creature blinded or without eyes have a more heightened sense to compensate. Meaning that even a slight change of pressure would be met with resistance due to curiosity and self-preservation.

Snaring those who can't see or make eye contact would involve gradually changing all the surrounding energy in an area to not draw attention to the coming control. That is likely how Kalt snared me last night. He might be used to using a snare skill. He had a short time from when he entered and when I realized I couldn't move. That also tells me that vampires can't sense another vampire's use of living energy. If it's done by stealthy means. In the case of a fly, it's hard to make direct eye contact. They can flee quickly if they sense danger. Changing the energy around a fly is the only way to snare it.

"Are we ready to give it a go?" Cronos asked Julia and me. We nodded.

Cronos opened the jar's lid. The flies flew in different directions. We each pointed to a fly to ensure no one accidentally snared the same one. When we each settled on who had which fly, we started working on our snare technique. Julia's fly was on the wall behind the bed's headboard. Cronos's fly was trying to hide among the books on a bookshelf. My fly was going after the bedroom light. I watched my fly's movements. I wanted to study it to decide what would be an appropriate amount of space to start snaring it. Then I saw that the fly was content with where it was. I started imagining the fly in a bubble. The bubble was slowly filled with more energy concentrated on the fly. Then I noticed that the fly I was watching started to fall from the light. I thought, no! Please move and fly somewhere! I hope I didn't kill it by accident! To my relief, the fly did move before it hit the ground and landed on the carpet beside me. Now how to see behind its eyes and tune into its senses?

It took some time for me to understand how snare worked. There was a difference between catching with a snare and controlling with a snare. Even then, maintaining control between the two seemed to be a different skill. From merely telling a creature what to do to be in that creature's mind as an observer. I notice the two other flies have come to visit mine. Julia and Cronos must have figured out how to control their flies. I feel bad. I still haven't learned how to connect with the fly's senses. After getting some encouraging words and suggestions from Julia and Cronos, I started seeing other visions.

This other vision only engulfed the edges of my vision, which was focused on the fly. It was like having a netted perception around my vision. Yet it made me feel sick. I closed my eyes and could still see what the fly saw. The change in scale and perception was still sickening. I tried to stop focusing on each eye's sight and only on the big picture: the floor with Julia and Cronos's flies beside mine. That perception shift helped.

I hear Cronos ask, "How do you feel, Roxanne?"

"I'm feeling better. I can see what the fly sees. Although I'll keep my eyes closed for now," I replied.

"If we're already, do we want to take our flies out to spy on the meeting? I think it would be good exercise. Even if we lose connection with our flies, it's not the end of the world. We can always ask how the meeting went later," Cronos proposed.

Julia and I thought it wouldn't hurt. Then Cronos went to open the door. I'm amazed that they had their eyes open while controlling a fly. They also can manage their own body long enough to open a door. I want to be able to do that someday, too. We sent our flies out of the room, and Cronos closed the door behind our flies. I see Julia's fly ahead of me. I only couldn't see Cronos's fly.

"Hey, where is your fly, Cronos?" I asked.

"My fly is just behind your fly, my little sister gem. I'll keep an eye on our rear to ensure we don't happen to meet any unwanted attention. Since we can't sense what they can, someone should linger behind. That is why watching in many directions as a group helps."

It felt like it took forever to get to the meeting room as a fly. The way that the fly moved while getting there was also sickening. So many angles, flying high and low out of the blue. Especially the big drops. It's like being on a roller-coaster that is free moving. There was no moment to brace for the sudden change. When we entered the meeting room, I had my fly rest on the nearest wall to collect myself.

"Do any of you feel sick after that?" I ask,

I pray I'm not the only one in the room who feels like puking.

"It really is a rough skill to master. I'm not feeling great either, Roxanne." I hear Julia say.

I opened one of my eyes out of curiosity. I couldn't help feeling that Julia and Cronos were experts at snare. I'm sure Julia was just her usual polite self. When I looked over at Julia, she did look a little paler. Still, she managed to look relaxed despite her discomfort. Julia might not have mastered snare, but she knows how to master hiding her uncomfortable feelings.

"Alright, try listening to what they're talking about with your flies," Cronos said quietly.

I think they must have already started to listen in on the conversation. Julia whispered a trick to help open my ears to listening in on the fly. I think she knew because it is similar to what she and Cronos told me I needed to do to see behind the fly's eyes. I focused my energy on my ears and thought about the fly's means of listening. I find it surprising that even though a fly hears sounds, it doesn't process our language like we do. So even though we are essentially making an animal listen to these people talk, it will only sound like noise to them. Despite that, we can hear words and conversations in real-time.

"Lord Sturm. I see that you have sent a request form for a move of transfer to Lord Van Kurt's clan. Yet I don't see the vampire's name the request is for. Could you explain more about the transfer being motioned for the council?" The lady in the black robes said.

Cronos's father stood up and adjusted his tie.

"Thank you for the honor of explaining. As you all know, finding a human with a gift to magnify living energy is rare. It's even more rare for two in less than two hundred years to be born in the same territory of our council's borders. Yet it has happened. My clan has found a gem in our clan's territory. Unlike the late Aria Rosewell, the young man's gift requires instruments then singing. Our clan has looked over him since he was a babe. The man is twenty-three years old and has been growing restless and confined to our territory. Since the young man desires change, we've felt it best to send him to the late Aria Van Kurt's venues to perform in the Van Kurt clan territory. We know that Lord Van Kurt is a capable and respectable man. He not only has history but more knowledge of human gems than any one clan leader here," Cronos's father said.

Before Lord Strum could make his case further, a man sitting next to Lady Van Schlager interrupted.

"If I may be so bold, Lord Strum. Isn't this request asking far too much of our Lord Van Kurt? The good man lost his dear wife only fourteen years ago. And you ask him to watch over and protect another so soon?" The man said with a tone of pity.

"I assure you it will not be Lord Van Kurt that we ask to be the young man's protector. Only Lord Van Kurt provides the opportunity for the young man in his territory. Also, we request that he guides the young man's new protector," Lord Strum replied.

"Who will you assign Lord Strum as the boy's protector?" Lady Van Schlager asked. While she seemed unfazed by this news, Kalt's look told a different story.

I can see the wheels turning behind Kalt's eyes from where my fly was on the wall. My thoughts went to the same place as his, I'm sure.

"We feel that despite her vampire age, the young Roxanne can grow into her father's shoes of being a proper protector for the young man. Mourning her mother's death would be different since she never really had much time with her. Roxanne also has more experience in human culture and behaviors than most vampires. From what I can see from yesterday's events, she is learning much of our vampire ways despite being so young. We feel that she would be the best option for his protector," Lord Strum said.

Kalt's eyes looked as cold as ice. So they're going to arrange for me to be with this human. Like the council arranged for my father to protect and marry my mother. Are the Strums trying to help me or hurt this young man? They should know that if anyone gets close to me, Kalt has clarified that he is their enemy. The man could die because he had the misfortune of having me as a protector. Or he could be used as leverage to ensure my own death by the lady who wants me dead.

4

The Plan

"Please forgive me for being out of line with this, Lord Strum," Kalt began to say.

"Hasn't the council agreed upon during yesterday's meeting that Roxanne Van Kurt is a bit young of a vampire to take on an adult responsibility? If I recall from yesterday's argument, the fact that she went feral shows her immaturity and emotional instability. How can she be expected to protect anyone if she can't control her emotions? Let alone her transformation is a mere cub. She can learn much from her father, but knowledge isn't enough when it comes to the task of a protector. Correct me if I'm wrong, but a protector's job is to protect. She'll need to have actual strength for the task at hand. I'm sorry, I don't see a mere cub as a powerful beast. Especially compared to Lord Van Kurt. I doubt she has it in her nature to fight when the time calls for it," Kalt continued.

Yeah, the same train of thought. Dad became a clan leader

because of his power and history of fighting. All he lacked was the knowledge required of a person in a leadership position. Moving the fight from a physical to an oral and written battle. My father believes I have strength. Yet like Kalt said, I don't see it in myself. Plus, I might wake my blood lust if I fight. I could have that hunger to kill like dad.

I do appreciate what the Sturm family is trying to do for me. However, I might have to agree with Kalt. Father surprised me by standing up. I thought that he would've chosen to stay out of the conversation. With a soft knowing look in his eyes and a light smile, it's clear father was confident in what he would do.

"You have pointed out some fair concerns, Kalt. Indeed, Roxanne hasn't had the experience yet to take on such a role as protector. However, you're wrong to think that she has no strength. It's true that a cub doesn't have the same power as a beast. Yet a child of a beast is still clever. That creativity and boldness have strength, too. Even threatened, a cub has fangs.

I know of a man with much less power than I had. He used to be the former leader of my clan. I lost a fight with him. When it came to knowledge and duty to protect others, even a man such as that is equal to me. Power is in the perception of those who choose to use it and not let themselves be consumed by it.

There are areas in which Roxanne has limitations. With time and experience, she will overcome them. She is powerful enough to try new things and experiment with the knowledge she has. When feeling threatened or cornered, she tries new skills if it means a chance of surviving. I will share with her what knowledge I do have. I know she'll take that knowledge and go much further with it than I can think to take it. She was raised by a family of scientists, after all. She has learned not to take facts without experimentation. Facts mean nothing if they cannot be proven true.

I learned from Julia yesterday that Roxanne has been experimenting with her new reality since her blood awoke. She has been learning what she can and can't do without permission. That curiosity and knowledge of safe experimentation gives her a unique strength few vampires have. She has already learned how sunlight affects her without hurting herself. Something I think most of us here would never consider doing. It would be seen as mad if anyone tried," father said.

He waited to see if anyone would respond to his case.

"If Roxanne chooses to accept or decline the role of protector for this boy, I'll support her. I choose to leave it to her and the council to decide," father finished saying before he sat back down in his chair.

I wonder if father said that last part because he is required to let the council have a say. I ponder what dad said about my ability and his friend, Emir. I reflect on the story of their fight. Is that the same power he believes I can offer my sisters if anything ever happens to him?

It hasn't dawned on me till now. There are many things I do that my sisters wouldn't do. Julia was bothered by my sunlight experiment. How they talk about illusions versus transformations made it seem like they don't find illusions useful; till now. However, I used one when I was being followed that one evening. I ask questions to learn more about my reality and test it in different situations. Whether the outcome isn't certain or before it's even considered necessary.

Each sister has their own gifts and strengths. Amelia is willing to try new things but often from existing ideas. She's a bit of a copycat. Julia knows how to keep her family safe, hidden, and healthy. August, like dad, knows political strategy laws and vampire culture.

Kalt will go after this human. I know it. He warned me as much during our conversation last night. Still, could I? Should I accept the role of protector if they decide to let me have a say?

"What if the boy gets it in his head that he could have a romantic relationship with her? What then would you do, Lord Van Kurt?" Kalt asked.

"Even though the boy has been looked after by the Sturm clan, he could think that Roxanne is old enough to marry," Kalt continued.

I watch those in the room becoming uncomfortable at this remark. The council members knew where this was heading.

"Don't pretend it was lost on us during yesterday's meeting. Orchestrating verbal permission to the sound clan leaders to be given permission to have a child. Knowing full well that the permission does extend to their children. Who of the sound clan leaders is going to have that permission?" Kalt asked, getting gradually angrier with each word.

"You're getting out of line, Kalt," an infected leader said.

"It's common knowledge that such matters are discussed by each sub-council. An example of this is if Lady D. Cargy continues to refuse to infect a successor. As leaders of the infected, we'll have to step in to ensure that her clan isn't left without guidance and order," this leader continued.

"Roxanne is a child to us. However, humans are only ever children," my father replied.

"Letting children be children doesn't cross any boundaries of ours. She'll undeniably outlive him. Whatever their relationship results in will be with sorrows in the end," father explained.

"Speaking from experience there, Lord Van Kurt?" Lord Sturm asked.

Father just smiled.

"I just trust my children to live their lives well. As Lord Foster said, it's up to the sub-councils to assign the right to have children, Kalt. Even if the man and Roxanne ask, it's not their decision or ours," father replied.

Kalt sat back in his chair, unhappy. I hear Cronos chuckle beside me.

"Did he really think he could intimidate them? To prevent you from having your own happy life?" Cronos asked.

I felt like I'd seen enough. I let my connection with the fly break to talk with Cronos.

"What are you talking about?" I asked.

"The friend I talked about last night is that gem that my clan will be transferred to your care. Even if your blood didn't wake this year, we still planned to send him to your father's territory. We wanted you and him to meet. Even if it meant some coaxing to get you out of your aunt and uncle's house. My family and I feel that you two would be a good match if allowed to meet. While we're strict about vampires marrying other vampires, the same can't be said if a vampire wants to marry a human. We also didn't know that Kalt would behave this way toward you.

Given that he has made it nearly impossible to have the option to fall in love with another vampire, he can't do a dam thing about this. That is if you and our gem decide to become something more. Also, if you look after him, Kalt has fewer opportunities to take him away from you or harm him. He is now under council protection if assigned to you," Cronos said with delight.

"So, the Sturm family is plotting my future, too?" I asked bluntly.

"Come now, little Roxanne. We won't force you to do anything you don't want to do. We only want to provide you with options for a happy life. At the very least, we want to offer you a friend who can relate better to you than most vampires. To have a friend who understands your love for music and shares your interest. Someone to share your creativity and passions with. You'll appreciate him when you meet him.

Your friends as a human were lovely and all. Except they barely connected with you and your interest. You would be surprised how nice it is to feel that someone understands rather than just being understood. I promise we'll not drag more expectations into the relationship than the two of you choose to have with each other," Cronos said.

Then Cronos chuckled and said, "But watching Kalt fret over it is fun."

Cronos and Julia are equally scary when it comes to keeping the family safe.

"I must ask, is this one of those times you consider yourself a ton of fun?" I asked, unsure what to expect Cronos to say.

"No, this is petty of me to poke fun of Kalt. I don't like when people I'm fond of are being mistreated. Since the matter is out of our hands, you can choose to have a life despite what Kalt has done. Now let's have some real tons of fun as a family," Cronos replied.

We heard a knock on the door while Cronos was pulling the cards out of their back pocket. Julia opened the door and saw August looking a little worried.

"I'm sorry to bother you all. The council wishes to talk with Roxanne," August said.

"Of course. Are you alright, August?" Julia asked.

"I'm worried about how things have escalated with Kalt. None of that matters now. I'll keep an eye on Roxanne as always," August said.

August has a fair reason to be afraid. August knows that if the man is under my care with how things are now, he'll become a target for Kalt. The other side of the coin is August doesn't know how such arrangements have historically affected our family. Even I'm a target for Kalt's mother. If she didn't hate me for being my mother's daughter, she'd hate me now for making her son look like a fool in front of the council. I got up from the floor and went to the door.

"Let's go meet with them then," I told August.

I put my arm around August's shoulders and said, "You don't need to worry. I won't be surprised by what they're likely going to ask. Cronos and Julia worked with me on some snare illusion."

"I know. We talked about its last night while you were in bed. Cronos told us more about the friend who would come to stay with us. Last night I thought it was a great idea. Now I don't know. Kalt was trying his best to prevent you from being his protector. I really wish I understood why he's acting this way. I'm afraid for that boy," August said quietly as we approached the council's meeting room.

"I understand. I'll not take this decision lightly. Can I ask that you trust in me a little?" I asked.

August looked over at me. She nodded and smiled.

"Of course, I'll trust you. But trust us too, okay," August replied.

I nodded with a smile.

I hate to tell August that, at the moment, I have no plan for responding. I only wanted to know that my family would accept my choice. Even if it causes me some type of pain in the future. I wondered what good could really come from being this human's protector. Perhaps there is more to this than even I had initially considered. But what? What could he have to offer beyond companionship and magnifying living energy?

We walked into the room and stood where our seats were yesterday. August told me through telekinesis that I needed to stay standing when we got to our seats. We couldn't sit because I was expected to speak. August will escort me out when we finish this conversation.

"Miss Roxanne Van Kurt," The lady in the black robe said, "We appreciate that you're willing to meet with the council on such short notice."

The lady then explained the events that transpired in a brief summary. During that time, I started to wonder what I wanted to do and my present limitations. What can a human do that I can't? And how can I keep a human safe? My mind was running to find an answer I felt I would be content to make.

"…. being said, we don't wish to force potentially dangerous work as a protector on you. We want your choice to be considered. Do you choose to be this human's protector?" The lady in the black robe asked.

I smiled and said, "I choose to take on the role of protector for this human."

I could feel the heat of tension in the air. I could feel the weight of Kalt's glare, but it didn't get to me. I know we'll have our conflicts and fights. It's inevitable. Even if I did choose to back down from this position. I understand that any human can be in danger. Even my old friends can be in trouble. I'll need to learn to protect people who matter to me. Now is an excellent time to start.

I must find my own answers to questions. Kalt said so himself last evening. A human assistant would help me find more clues to the past. A helper who can go to places my mother went and places I cannot reach because I'm not human anymore.

"Thank you for your prompt response, Roxanne. We, the council, trust you to take the role of protector seriously. It's your council's assigned task from this day forward till the death of the man or yourself. Since the man is officially assigned by the council body, we will present proof of your role.

Not right now. It will be after the meeting. It's the official seal of the protector. It will be given to Lord Van Kurt to be given to you officially. We'll trust your father, Lord Van Kurt, to educate you further on what the seal offers you and the one under your care," The lady in the black robe said almost dismissively.

I nodded and thanked them.

August walked me out of the meeting space to return to Julia's room. She looked wearily at me.

'Is being a protector what you want to do?' she asked telepathically.

It's a little late to be asking this. That and August said she would trust me.

"It's likely Kalt would have tried to target him regardless out of fear. Worse yet, He could have tried to offer to be the human's protector. Then we'd have no clue what could happen to him. At least this way, we'll know the human is safe. Plus, Cronos and their family trust us. I don't think they would have offered if they didn't think it was worth the risk. They care about the boy," I said in a hushed tone.

Though I said all of this more for myself. I wish I could feel less guilty for wanting the human to help me solve my personal mystery.

'Your right. We don't know how Kalt will respond either way. The boy could be in danger, regardless. If Kalt sees him as a threat, the boy could die silently, and no one would ever know he died,' August thought.

"Alright, we'll help you look after him," she said reassuringly.

"Hu?" I said out of surprise.

'A protector is often older than a few days old vampires. Since you're still learning a lot, we'll help look after him. Until you're able to look after him properly,' she thought.

Well, this isn't a part of the plan. I should've guessed that this could have happened. My sisters want to support me. It's only natural that they'd want to take on the part of my role because they see me as a child. Well, fuck me. How will I ask the human to find information for me if they're going to keep an eye on us? I don't want my family to worry about my desire to know more about my past.

Dad doesn't know. My sisters would know even less. Probably? I never thought of asking them if they knew my mother. I wonder how my mother felt meeting them. She probably felt strange looking as old as dad's children. Yet knowing their hundreds of years older than her.

When we return to Julia's room, August's spirits look lifted. Even Julia seemed mildly confused about why August was so happy when she opened the door to meet us. Despite this, Julia smiled gently and greeted us with a welcome back. Cronos was grinning from ear to ear. August had to excuse herself and head back to the meeting.

"I suppose it has all turned out well, given August's demeanor," Julia said.

"It has. Haven't you and Cronos been observing the meeting through the flies?" I asked.

"I did observe. Julia lost connection when August came to get you. I told her what happened, minus a few parts," Cronos explained,

"Anyway, I am glad you agreed to protect him, little Roxanne. I know you'll love him and be quick friends in no time," Cronos cheered.

"Yes, I think it is great that you'll have a friend now," Julia said.

"I'm a little worried about Kalt's behavior. However, it's a comfort to hear that you seemed to hold your own when he tried to make a scene," Julia explained.

"Yes, you looked epic," Cronos practically sang with delight.

"I would be lying to say it doesn't concern me. Even if I caved and didn't agree, Kalt could still go after this human. At least this way, we can form a defense between him and Kalt," I explained.

Cronos nods.

"You're clever little Roxanne," they said with pride.

"That's true. Father will teach you well. I'm positive you can learn fast. Until you're better enabled, we can also help lend a hand to keep this person safe," Julia said.

She seemed more content with this idea.

"August said the same thing before we got here. She was worried about all of this, too," I said.

"Well, let's leave Kalt in the past. I can't wait to tell Gabriel the good news when we return home today," Cronos cheered.

"So, this human's name is Gabriel? I think I should know his name since I'll guard him from now on," I asked.

"That's right. Your new friend's name is Gabriel Maxwell," Cronos answered.

"The council often doesn't ask for names of humans to

help aid their official protector. Everyone knows your mother by name and that your father was her protector. That was because the council was informed about her pretty late. Apparently, she used to perform everywhere she could before your father was assigned to be her protector. As a result, many clans claimed her. They didn't know that she traveled between territories at the drop of a hat. Only when some clans appointed protectors to follow her did they learn all this. The case became a council matter of concern. Simply put, your father had to reel your mother into one place for her safety.

From what I heard, he created many places within his territory for her. That way, she would never feel bored and always have an opportunity to work. I know Gabriel will be happy to meet another gem like you, Roxanne," Cronos explained.

"I get why you call Gabriel a gem. He has a favorable talent that vampires love. But why are you calling me a gem when my mother had the favorable talent? Or is everyone a gem to you? I can surely understand my sister Julia being a gem in your eyes," I asked.

"No, No. My fair lady Julia is the queen of my heart, worth more to me than any gem, little sister Roxanne," Cronos said poetically.

They kissed Julia sweetly.

Then they continued, "There was a time when some members of my family's clan watched over you while you were two years old. We know first-hand that you have your mother's special talent for singing. It wouldn't surprise me that Kalt knows of this talent of yours since some of your friends live in that bloody territory.

When you were in preschool, your mother sent you to a school in my family's territory. You used to sing with her all the time as a little one. You used to sing to your teachers and classmates, too. While learning who was around you, we learned that you're a gem like your mother. Our clan members love you and your mother. We never knew a half-blood could inherit their gem parent's gifts until you came into our lives.

That is why we want to send Gabriel your way. You can have the joy you once had when your mother was alive. We want you to be happy like that again. Not all the clans know, nor will they learn your secret talent. Now that your blood is awake, your secret is better protected. Your aunt and uncle showed you great love for keeping your talent secret. Though they'll never know it."

I felt weird after hearing this. How could I have inherited my mother's talent? Or was it that they hoped that I would have my mother's talent. Now I'm learning that I have her talent. People knew it without telling me. Really? This is the same as when dad told me I'm likely an immortal like him. Perhaps he already knows somehow that I am one. I might be jumping to assumptions here, but this is nuts.

It's sweet of the Sturm clan to want me to be happy like I used to be. Yet, they still don't see this as history repeating itself. They only see and desire the history they remember that brought them joy. Is it for this Gabriel's good, though? Is this even what he wants? I want to be happy, but I feel conflicted. I know I'll make the most of the situation, but I can't say it's for his good.

I thanked Cronos for the thoughtful gift of being able to

have a friend soon. Julia seemed happy, too. We spent the rest of the time playing card games and telling jokes. Before we knew it, August was back to let us know that the meeting had ended. We got our belongings and parted ways with Cronos. They had to return to their family's home to get their belongings together to move to our home. I don't see how we would fit in my mother's house. Father seemed to think the same thing and told Cronos to send their belongings to our family's mansion. Apparently, we'll be moving back sometime soon.

5

Side Effects Included

The walk back home felt like it took less time than going to the Van Schlager mansion. I honestly couldn't say for sure how I was feeling. I'm glad to still be with my family. I'm happy to have met Cronos. I'm looking forward to seeing them again in a few months. I'm thrilled to be in my familiar home and see Amelia again. I hope that she has been well while we're gone. I can't imagine what she's been up to. I can sleep without the fear of being snared again or having to watch my back every minute. I should be happy.

Despite these things, I'm not happy. I can't dismiss this shadow-like feeling cast over my mood. I'm away from danger. Why do I still feel like trouble is following me? I thought I knew who my problem was. I have learned that more people are trying to plan my life or kill me. I'm trying to make the most of my options. Although, I still feel I've less control over my life.

Having people plan out my future was what I've been through while living with my aunt and uncle. I know I'm young for a vampire, but I want to be seen as a grown-up. That way, I can feel less threatened and controlled by others. My family has been helping me and caring for me. I'm thankful for that, but I need something more. Something that no vampire can manipulate, control, or decide for me. I wish I could spend time with my old friends. I don't know how easy or hard it'll be to see them again when we move.

We see Amelia running out the front door to greet us when we arrive home. She looked like a wild person with her untamed hair. She tried to hug all of us at once. Sadly, she could only get Julia and me into her embrace. August ended up giving her an assuring pat on her shoulder. Father waited until Amelia gave August a proper hug before she could hug him.

"How did everything go?" Amelia asked.

Amelia was clinking to our father, who didn't seem to mind.

"Everything when well, considering how the council usually turns out," father replied.

He looked happy but sounded tired. I think that even today's meeting took a lot out of him.

"Julia and Cronos are officially engaged to be married," August said.

August still presented herself with more energy compared to our father. Perhaps this type of work energizes her compared to dad. Or it could be because she doesn't have to talk as much as our father does. Who knows?

"That's wonderful! Congratulations, Julia!" Amelia said, going back to hug Julia.

"Thank you, Amelia," Julia said with a motherly smile.

"Will we be seeing Cronos later this evening?" Amelia asked

"No," I replied.

"Cronos must get their belongings together and send it to our family mansion. They'll not be arriving any time soon," I said.

"Cronos will also be bringing a friend for Roxanne," Julia chimed.

Amelia looked over at me with her eyes lit up.

"That's exciting. Do we know this person?" Amelia asked.

"We haven't met them yet, my dear Amelia," father sighed.

He was passively trying to encourage us to finish our walk home. He didn't seem to mind the idea of us talking along the way. As we started to follow him, August continued to explain what happened yesterday and this morning to Amelia.

"That's dirty of that sick man," Amelia growled.

She tried to hug me as we walked.

"Why would he try to go and make a scene like that in front of everyone?" Amelia asked.

"We're not sure. It could be Kalt's attempt to keep Roxanne single even when she does come of age to marry our kind properly," August explained.

"Despite that, Cronos feels that this gifted person named Gabriel could be a good friend for Roxanne. We can have peace knowing that our Roxanne will not be lonely for these next few decades. Plus, with the title of a council-appointed protector, she can continue to look after any rare human she wishes for years to come. If desired, she can marry them," Julia explained to Amelia.

"Hum... I hadn't even thought about that. The council seems protective of father not being asked to look after this human," I said as we entered the front door of our house.

I then noticed that August and Julia handed their bags over to Amelia. I was about to put my bag down when Amelia grabbed it from my hand. Father didn't hand over his bag and started heading upstairs. Amelia followed a few steps behind him.

When they were both out of earshot, I said, "That's odd."

"What is?" August asked.

"What Amelia did. It seemed odd to me," I replied.

"That's just what we do," August said, still confused by my confusion.

Julia giggled at the situation.

"It's an unspoken family tradition. We've always thought it considerate in our family that whoever didn't go to council meetings would show hospitality to the ones who attended. When I was an only child and used to attend council meetings, our mother always took our bags from us when we got home. Amelia learned from our mother to collect our bags after we returned from council meetings. She has been doing this since she was a young child. When August was born and able to attend as our father's successor, I also learned this custom of care in our family. I bet that Amelia would've liked to be able to carry all four of our bags. Father's gesture made it clear that care should be shown to us. He planned to manage his own." Julia reminisced.

I missed the gesture Julia was referring to that told Amelia not to collect dad's bag. August seemed surprised by what Julia told us. She must have thought it was a common thing people do. It's easy to forget why acts of kindness and love go unnoticed nowadays. We get so used to experiencing another's love we never consider it.

I also never thought of it since August is our father's successor. There was a time Julia would've been considered our father's successor when she was born. Julia was his first child. There was no guarantee that a vampire could have many children. At least, that is what I have learned from this meeting. There is a lot of red tape to have a child.

I wonder if there was a time when she was expected to be our father's successor? Julia appears to be content not having that role. From what I can see, she seems supportive of August as our father's successor. She looks up to her mother and wants to be like her for us.

"That was very kind of your mother to do," I said.

"I think so, too," Julia replied with a smile.

"It will be one of your jobs from now on, too, Roxanne," Amelia said, coming down the stairs in a hurry.

"Having a human to look after will not get you out of your share of family responsibilities," she continued.

"I suppose I'll have to learn a lot about what we do behind the scenes from you next, Amelia," I replied thoughtfully.

"Yep, and nothing you say will get you out of it," Amelia said in a mix of a playful and severe tone.

"First, the basics of being a vampire. Then she can go with

you to work," August said. "Roxanne still can't use her tele-kinesis properly," August continued to justify her case.

"Come on, like it will take a long time for Roxanne to learn," Amelia huffed.

"How about we get your hair done, Roxanne?" Julia asked to change the subject.

Deflecting the tension as usual. I can understand a bit more why Julia got good at it.

"Sure. Long hair is nice, but it does feel like a little extra weight on my shoulders." I said half-jokingly.

Perhaps a haircut could help lift some of my negative feelings. I might feel better with a lighter head of hair again. Julia smiled. We went into the kitchen like the last time. The conversation moved with us. It continued well after Julia fixed my hair into a lovely pixie mohawk. Father showed up a few minutes after that and joined in.

We eventually migrated back to the living room. Everyone tried to help me learn how to control my telekinesis. They thought it would be easier for me to try controlling my tele-kinesis in my human form. By the time the sun started rising, we were all talking to each other by telekinesis. It was fun and tiring. We made a point to eat well before bed.

It was heaven to be back in my own bed. I hoped that I could dream again. Perhaps see that strange child again. I might feel a little bit better if I knew what the warning was about.

I didn't have a dream that night, to my disappointment. I just remembered the look on Kalt's face when I told the coun-cil that I would agree to protect this human. I wasn't scared at the time. Now, I can't help but feel intimidated. His eyes were colder than usual. It felt like he had more power than me at that moment. I feel small. Can I really protect Gabriel from Kalt?

I get myself ready for a new day. At least I have my family to help. I still wish I could send him to find some information about my mother's death. Well, take one day at a time.

Kalt might be a pureblooded vampire, but that only means he comes from a family that bred a lot. He should then be a lot weaker than me in comparison. Since the only vampire blood I have is from an immortal, I'm naturally stronger, and my skills with time will grow sharper. That thought puts a part of my mind at ease.

Overall, I still can't help feeling concerned. What would help relieve my tension would be finding out what possible danger the child mentioned. I don't dream. I can't ask her out of the blue. I wonder if it's a warning about Kalt or this human. My mind is jumping from one concern back to another. I wish it would stop.

Okay, get yourself together. I can only manage what is before me. I should do my best today and learn how to help this boy. I went downstairs and into the living room. Father was awake and sitting in his usual chair with a book.

'I see that your awake, my dear Roxanne, ' father said through his telekinesis with me.

'Morning, father! Why are you using your telekinesis this early in the morning?' I asked with my own telekinesis.

'Because I want to talk with you about something that has been bothering me since yesterday's meeting," father thought.

'That look you gave Kalt when you accepted to look after the boy is one I know well. Your mother would make that face when she thought she was being clever. When she was about to do something reckless,' father continued to think.

'You want to know what I was thinking during that time?' I wondered with my father.

'No, I know you'll do what is expected of you as the boy's protector. I will warn you that I'll intervene if you put the boy's life in danger out of reckless desires. You're as much her child, too. I know the temptation to find answers about your mother is alluring. But that boy isn't a tool. He is a living being, Roxanne. Never forget that while he's in your care,' father finished his thoughtful lecture.

"We have some work to do these next few days. We'll need your help getting ready to move back to our family mansion, Roxanne," father said allowed.

I said nothing.

I felt angry that my father scolded me for something I hadn't done...yet. It's not like I've intentionally planned to endanger the boy. I just needed a personal reason to agree to look after him. What little confidence do they place in me? The council can scheme over my life, and I can't decide things for myself. What a load of bull crap.

"What is it, my child?" father asked.

'I'm sick of how it feels like everyone in the council has an agenda for me. Is it wrong to have a personal reason for wanting to go along with an others plan?' I asked by telekinesis.

'Having a reason isn't wrong, but it is wrong if you put that boy in danger,' he shared his thoughts with me again.

"When must we get things ready for the move?" I decided to say to change the subject.

"We'll start packing this evening. I'll also spend some time talking to you about the basics of the job of protector before dawn," father replied.

My sisters showed up and started talking about what the mansion looked like to me. It sounds like what I'd expect a vampire's house to look like. Our mansion has many rooms like the Van Schlager mansion. I was told I could pick out my room when we moved in. That should be fun. Each of my sisters preoccupies rooms in different corners of the mansion. There is a beautiful garden in the backyard with flowers representing something special. Yet my sisters wouldn't tell me more about the garden. They said it would be a surprise when we were home.

We had our breakfast and then started getting our rooms packed. The process felt like I was getting nowhere fast. It may not have helped that I wondered what I could do about finding information. Since I couldn't ask the human for help, thanks to dad. I've been wondering about snaring an animal to hunt down information.

The thing is, I haven't quite mastered snare yet. Depending on the animal, I might find limitations to what kind of information I can gather. Hell, I don't know where to start looking for information about my mom. Where would I even start looking for a clue? I continued to ponder this question while packing until my mind began to wander.

It took a paper cut from the box I was packing to snap out of my mindless trance. I stopped what I was doing to find a first aid kit in the bathroom. When I opened the medicine cabinet door, I reflected on what dad mentioned the night he found me. He found me in a secret space in this house. Some place I could fit in. A spot a four-year-old can hide without people being able to find them. If I find that place, perhaps I can remember what happened to mom.

The only thing is that I've been through this whole house. I haven't found anything odd that a child could hide in. Didn't dad also say he fixed that spot before I arrived? What could a child get into that would need to be fixed? Perhaps that can be my next test with a snare. Find a fly or bug that can freely wander the house to find crevices. If I search carefully, I might find something a child could hide in. I'll need to see it before we leave. Otherwise, I doubt father would let me return here to continue looking.

That's it, then. I'll work on that while trying to tame this packing business. I finished dressing my cut and went back to my room. Now to find a bug to snare and perhaps a jar to store them.

Thankfully it didn't take long for a moth to show up at my window. I used a snare to bring the moth inside my room. Now to find a jar to keep it in. I looked through the vanity drawer again to see if there was anything I could use to help. No dice. Okay, plan B. I'll just need to catch a bug each day while 'packing to help me explore the nooks and crannies of this house. That isn't bad. Just a bit more of a challenge.

With my mind made up, I snared the moth again. I looked behind its eyes and helped navigate it around my room. I moved boxes to make sure we didn't miss anything. I packed small things that needed to be moved. The moth was better enabled to move around with more space.

Still, we couldn't find anything unusual in my room. Great, one room down and no sign of a clue. I heard a knock on my bedroom door. It breaks my connection with the moth. I went to open the door to find Julia standing there.

"I wanted to let you know that we just got the good news. Your sound stone will be ready for pick up tomorrow," Julia said sweetly.

"That's great! It still feels uncomfortable sharing everyone's sound stone to eat from. I can't bring myself to eat much from the blue heart sound stone," I replied.

"I understand. It's not easy to share food. I can also imagine that Kalt's gift would be hard to eat from," Julia empathized with me.

"Speaking of that thing, I'll be heading out to gather energy for us. Would you mind if I brought it along while hunting?" Julia asked.

"No, it's not a problem," I said, handing her the blue heart sound stone.

"I wonder what my new sound stone will look like," I said.

"I'll not be the one to tell you that. You'll have to wait until tomorrow to see for yourself," Julia replied playfully.

"Will Amelia be picking it up tomorrow? Will I be able to go with her if she does?" I asked.

"We'll wait until tomorrow before making that decision. It will likely be Amelia picking up your new sound stone," Julia said.

I grinned and said, "I hope I can go and see it."

"You'll know tomorrow, my curious little sister," Julia said.

"I want to bring Roxanne to pick it up tomorrow," Amelia says from her room.

"We're not encouraging this behavior, Amelia. We'll know tomorrow what the plan is. It depends on what we can get done today," Julia replied.

"But I want to take Roxanne with me when I go out tomorrow. I haven't been able to spend much time with her as you all have. It's my turn to spend time with Roxanne," Amelia huffed.

"You'll be showing her the ropes of what our family does when we're not dealing with politics soon, Amelia," Julia tried to reason with her.

Amelia went silent. Likely brewing over not knowing if she can bring me with her tomorrow.

"I better check in on her. Anyway, we'll know what the plan is tomorrow. For now, if you don't mind," Julia said with her hand stretched out.

"O' right," I said.

I just remembered that she wanted to take my old sound stone.

"I suppose I should be grateful that we have much to look forward to in the next few days," I say.

"It'll be a lot of changes. Don't let the stress of all of it get to you. You have us going through it with you, too," Julia assured me.

"By the way, would you like me to deal with that moth for you?" Julia asked.

"What?" I said, looking back into my room.

The moth was flying at the room's light, trying to get at it. Without another word from me, Julia snared the moth and brought the bug to her hand.

"Thank you for that, Julia," I said.

Julia smiled, taking both my sound stone and the moth with her. She is getting better at her snare illusion. I closed the door to my room. So much for having a bug help me search for a clue. Since I didn't know where to look, I continued cleaning my room.

After a few hours, I hear father call me. I went into the living room to find him. He is still sitting in his usual chair and asked me to sit beside him. I can't say my mood since this morning has improved. Yet I understand what he was trying to get across to me. Just because humans can be helpful doesn't mean they should be treated with any less respect than anyone else. Until eleven days ago, I thought I was human. For my entire life, I have been under the protection of my vampire family. Why would I expect my family to offer this new human any less care?

"How are you feeling after our conversation this morning?" he asked me.

"I've had time to think about it, and you are right. I will never let the human get in any danger. I was being thoughtless. I just don't what everything in my life to be decided for me by other vampires," I replied.

"I am glad that you're considering his welfare. You would also be in danger if you did put him in danger. That is the last thing I want you to be in. You'll learn that lesson early as a protector, my Roxanne. Humans don't often understand our limitations as vampires and only know us for our power and strengths. He will view you as powerful and do one of two things. He would either listen to you or risk putting himself in danger because he knows you'll protect him.

That was the first lesson I had to learn from your mother. She didn't understand that there were times and places I couldn't keep her as safe as I would like to. For our first year of me watching her, she would go places that tested the boundaries of where I could go. Constantly testing what she could do without arguing with me," father said.

"You think this boy will be as reckless as mother was?" I asked.

"It's possible. This human may have time to learn about vampires from the Sturm family. Because we're a new family of vampires looking out for his welfare, he might try to push his luck. He might want to see what he can get away with doing under our watch," father replied.

"Now, my dear child. Are you ready for your first lesson as a protector?" he asks me.

6 |

Friends or Phantoms

Father taught me what he had learned during his first year looking after my mother. Primarily we focused on locations. He felt that I needed to understand our territory and its secrets. He also shared what information we had on neighboring territories. That information was limited to only public knowledge. Father assured me that our information was enough to operate with care.

Father occasionally left his chair to get maps from the bookshelf. He had maps from 50-plus years ago. Old and new building blueprints with specific layouts in mind. He even had maps of plans in progress for zoning and construction work. He also had some proposed building plans submitted not yet approved to our territory's governing body. It really shouldn't surprise me that he can find this information. He has many connections that I still don't understand. I can't help but find myself fascinated.

Father discussed how planning and strategizing places to go in emergencies is essential. How to avoid being seen. Areas to consider hiding should the sun come out before we return. Plus, how to make it back to the mansion in an emergency. He told stories of his experiences of having to hide while the sun was up with my mother.

"It naturally worried your sisters," father concluded.

"I can see that. You had us worried when you confronted Kalt about his behavior," I said.

"I'm an old vampire and had a lot of time to learn many survival tricks. In the past, my mind had to work more on the fly when surviving a mad world. We can plan for future events thanks to technology, zoning laws, and other factors. Events that we have never considered beforehand. Don't ever take that for granted, my dear Roxanne. You girls don't have to worry about my safety as much. However, I do appreciate knowing that I'm loved by my family," father replied.

It was a lot of information to take in for one evening. I couldn't help but take in every word father said. The maps fascinated me. His stories delighted me because they were about my mom. I've often heard about my sister's mother and only pieces of my mom's life. It means a lot to have this time to learn how my mom was. I heard stories of places where she used to perform her music. Seeing the layout of those buildings made it feel like I was able to be a part of their story. Father also talked about the buildings he had made in his territory just for mom.

After that, my father and I discussed possible situations I could find myself in while caring for Gabriel. We talked for an hour. It got to a point where Julia and Amelia came into the living room to listen to our conversation. When August arrived, all three of us were pondering over a possible story of being prevented from leaving a parking lot at dawn.

"What is this about?" August asked.

"Training for Roxanne," father answered.

"How about an illusion to distract the person. Then transformation into a bat to fly into the nearest window?" Amelia suggested.

"But the sunlight could risk breaking the illusion. Plus, a bat flying at that time of day would confuse the person," Julia said.

"Any thoughts, Roxanne?" father asked.

"It should be okay not to use energy if the person is human. Walking away would be the quickest solution. Even if they're long-winded talkers. It reminds me of what August's said when she taught me how to hunt. We can stay or leave a conversation as we see fit. All we need to focus on is getting out of the sunlight," I answered.

"What if the person were armed with a weapon and threatening you?" father asked.

"I'd give them a piece of my mind!" Amelia said.

"That would only encourage the violence, Amelia." Julia retorted.

"It would be preferable to get distance away from them. Finding shelter would be a priority," August said.

"How would you girls accomplish that?" father asked.

August looked confused.

"What do you mean how?" August asked.

"Given the parking lot on this map, I think creating a distraction could be possible. It could create an opportunity to flee and find shelter. It's a loose gravel lot. Depending on whether the human can keep them distracted, I could hit these trash bins by throwing a rock. I point to the map where the trash bins are located. We could flee for this side alley when the person turns their head. I could hide us with an invisibility illusion since the sunlight won't be able to reach us at that time of day. After the person leaves, we can find shelter," I suggested.

"That could work in a particular situation. I'll encourage you to keep reflecting on it. Is that alright with you, Roxanne? You've done very well, and this type of situation would be a challenge for any of us," father said.

"It's getting to be dawn now. We best be getting to bed ourselves, girls," he continued.

"Wait!" Amelia cried out.

"Can Roxanne go with me to pick up her sound stone tomorrow?" she asked.

Father nodded with a smile.

"Yes, Roxanne may go with you tomorrow, Amelia. Letting Roxanne see more of our territory in person would be good. It would give her a chance to think about how to respond as a protector in that part of town," father said.

I made a discussed face at father.

"Really? You're assigning homework for tomorrow's outing?" I teased.

"Better than another lecture," father said.

"I honestly don't mind the lectures," I replied.

Amelia looked upset.

"I'm not saying being with you would be any less fun," I assured her.

"I just like father's stories," I continued.

"It's not often I talk about your mother with you," he said, seeming to understand.

"Time for bed, my dear girls. I will see you when night falls," father says sweetly.

We went to our rooms, and I got myself ready for bed. Feel excited at the thought of possibly being in a dream space again. I can't help wondering if I'll see that strange girl tonight.

She didn't appear again. I didn't have a single dream. That's two nights in a row now. Could my mind possibly prevent me from seeing her? It doesn't help that I don't know much about her. Nor do I know anything about the 'dream world' she made for us to converse in last time. All I have is a theory but no facts. I don't even know if she is a vampire or something else. She knows something and wants to warn me about it. I feel my mind running in circles, thinking of what her warning could be. Still, I won't know until we meet again. All I can does is assume until she tells me.

Before I knew it, I heard feet on the hardwood floors making sounds outside my room. Then I heard a door close. Next, there was a pounding sound.

"Oh, come on, Julia! You know I need to get ready early! I don't have time for this today," August's voice said.

I felt concerned and got out of bed to see what August was upset about. She was standing outside and pounding on the bathroom door.

"What is going on?" I asked August.

"Julia's getting into her old habit of dolling up. She used to spend hours doing who knows what to make herself look more appealing for Cronos. It stops each year around your birthday for a few weeks. Now she is back at it again," August answered.

"Okay. I thought I heard you say something about today being important?" I probed.

"Yes, today is the sub-council meeting. All future leaders meet to decide how to implement the motions made by the council. They also address local concerns for our types," August said while knocking on the door.

"All future leaders, even Kalt?" I asked.

"Thankfully, no. Sub-councils are like what the council used to be in old times. Sound vampires have their own sub-council. Blood eaters have their sub-councils. Infected vampires have their own. I'll meet with the other sound vampires concerning the finer details the council doesn't do. We'll determine who has permission to have children, adopt new plans to keep our clan-owned business legal, and other such topics. I don't feel like talking about it now. I promise I will tell you how things go today when I return. Now I want to get ready to head out with my father. Julia, get the fucking hell out of there already!" August said.

Julia finally opened the door.

"You don't need to take that tone with me. I have a right to get ready for the day as much as you do," Julia said hotly to August.

"What do you have to get ready for? Cronos will not be

here for a few more weeks. All you have to do is to help pack boxes for our move back home," August said out of frustration.

Before Julia could reply, August went into the bathroom and slammed the door shut. Julia stormed off downstairs. I felt stunned. I want to say I've never seen this side of them before, but that's not true. The last time August got angry with Julia was when she met Cronos the evening after my blood woke. I wonder if this is normal for them too. I went back to my room to get dressed.

I begin to wonder what my new sound stone will look like. I hope it looks cool, like Amelia's four-point star sound stone. Perhaps something like August's shark tooth sound stone. Julia's is elegant but not my style. Dad's sound stone is a classic oval jewel cut on a brooch he can pin to his tie. That wouldn't be my style, but I wouldn't mind it as much. It's a classic look. If I could choose my stone, it would be a lightning bolt, a crescent moon, or an X shape. Before I met Kalt, I would've considered a bat shape stone. However, I don't care for bats now. That reminds me, I never learned how to transform into a bat. I wonder if they'll get around to it sometime soon. Before my thoughts could wander any further, I heard knocking on my bedroom door.

"Roxanne, are you awake? Do I need to get the tuba?" Amelia asked from the other side of the door.

"I'm up, Amelia. You don't need to get the tuba out," I replied.

I adjust my gray sweater with one hand and open the door with the other.

"You need to comb your hair. The back is quite a mess," Amelia said bluntly.

I look at Amelia's hair. Her hair was just as untamed. I wonder if she is serious when she says stuff like this.

"I will. Would you like me to comb your hair while I'm at it?" I ask, thinking that she will flee as usual.

To my surprise, Amelia said, "Sure. You can't be any worse than Julia or my mother."

"Wait? Are you serious?" I asked.

"Yes. I let father and August brush my hair. But only when they're not busy with work," Amelia replied.

"Then why don't you comb your own hair?" I asked, sounding breathless.

"I don't care if my hair is messy," Amelia said.

I didn't know what to say after that. Amelia is such a free yet complicated spirit. Why does she then care how I look if she doesn't care how she looks?

"If we're done here, grab a comb. We'll have breakfast with the others. I can't wait to show you around town today!" Amelia chimed.

Amelia made her way downstairs. When I managed to collect myself after that discussion, I grabbed a comb and went to find the others in the living room. Julia and August seemed to be doing their best to ignore each other. I guess they're still upset about the bathroom conflict. I notice that father seems aware but chooses to stay out of it. He meets me with a warm smile while I quickly brush my hair. I sat next to Amelia. When I started combing Amelia's hair, Julia looked surprised.

"How did you get Amelia to let you comb her hair?!" she asked.

"I offered to comb her hair, and she decided to give me a chance," I replied.

I think Julia wouldn't want to know the extended version, especially with how this evening started for her.

"So, August has to go to the sub-council meeting today," I said to change the subject.

"Will it be as long as the council meeting we attended?" I ask.

"In the past, it used to take a week. Since we moved to this country, the sub-council has managed to keep meetings within six hours. I'll also be accompanying August at this meeting. I am an observer and help ensure that standard order is followed. This meeting is good practice for when August takes over as head," father explained.

"Sadly, it's not as open to the public as the council meetings are. Otherwise, I would like for you to see what we get to do, Roxanne," August said.

"It's okay, August. You can tell me how it went when you get back," I assured her.

"Speaking of which, you're going out with Amelia today. I want you to tell me what you notice while being out today. What would you do if you and the boy found yourselves in danger in that part of town?" father said.

"I know. Knowledge can only go so far without applying practical use. That makes the difference between head knowledge and practical knowledge," I reply.

Again, father smiles.

"Roxanne can have fun today, too. It doesn't always have to be work," Amelia said, sounding upset.

"Sometimes work can feel like play, Amelia. I think Roxanne can learn that best from you today," father said warmly.

I finish combing Amelia's long hair in time to see her smiling back at our father. Breakfast seemed brief. Julia finished and left the living room first. Dad and August left shortly after that. Then when Amelia was ready to go, we left to meet the cold fall air.

As we walked out of the cul-de-sac, Amelia started a conversation that was hard to follow. It had something to do with when she and the others lived in Germany. I didn't feel like asking her why she was telling me about Germany. She was so invested in telling her story. All I could do was follow along as best as I could. Perhaps it could be that she unknowingly used some German words to tell the story. When I couldn't follow a point in her story, I focused on the activity around us. Amelia talked about a horse that she got to ride in Germany when I saw two familiar faces that caused my heart to leap with joy.

It was Penny and Damian two blocks ahead of us. It looks like they're arguing over something. My curiosity got the best of me. I must know what's going on with my friends. I have to know what's happened to Sasha and Bruce. I looked around for anything that could help me get closer to them without being with them. I think this area was on the maps yesterday. There is a dumpster next door to that building Penny just entered. It sounds gross, but the dumpster would have a fly to snare.

"If you want some time to check in on them, you can," Amelia said out of nowhere.

I look over and see Amelia watching me.

"I don't mind giving you some time to check in on them. All we have to do today is pick up a package at the store. The store won't give us a hard time being late for anything." Amelia continued to explain.

I see she is talking in code like Kalt and August did during the night at the park. I suppose she doesn't want people to know we'll pick up the sound stone at...the store? This might not be as much of a code as I thought. I smiled and thanked Amelia.

We walked to where the dumpster was. I tentatively explained my idea to Amelia. First, we would check for any cameras nearby. Between the two of us, we found three cameras in the area. Amelia asked me what I was going to do. I told her about an electrical disturbance illusion that could work. In her bat form, Amelia can take to the sky to keep an eye out for any people coming my way. While she's in the sky, I can use a snare illusion to catch flies and spy on my friends in the store.

"I'm not an expert, but the cameras will see you if the illusion breaks. It's easy to lose focus between managing two different-natured illusions simultaneously?" Amelia argued.

"True. Then it'll be to help hide you while I try something else," I said.

"Like what?" Amelia asked.

"I read about a visual illusion to change my appearance to those who see me. I don't need to talk to my old friends.

I'll just listen to what they're arguing about as a simple bystander who is window shopping. That's why if my illusion does break, the chances of them seeing me will be slim to none," I said.

"Still seems risky to me. You should be okay if you can keep your distance. Don't forget about keeping out of sight of security cams," Amelia said.

I began to create an electronic disruption illusion on the three cameras. Amelia transformed and hid as I requested. I don't think Amelia would simply let me go without a pair of eyes watching me. I'm not going to worry about it. It's Amelia's right to look after me. Besides, I'm not trying to hide that I want to check on my friends from her. I have her support on this.

I create an illusion of what I want people around me to see me as. I look like an older woman with a bun of gray hair, a walking cane, and a hand-knitted shawl around my hunched shoulders. I make my way back to the front of the store. As I entered the shop, it didn't take long to find them next to the office supplies section of the store. I listen to them from the next row over. To not look like a stalker, pretending to be interested in the various options for printer paper.

"None of this would've ever happened if Roxanne never existed," Penny said hotly to Damian.

"Penny, that's enough. Voxy had nothing to do with what Bruce did to Sasha. Okay. No one but Bruce is responsible for his own actions that evening. I admit Sasha did agree to the drink. But she didn't know that my cousin would've drugged her drink. At the end of the day, Bruce got fired for what he did. We learned the law of cause and effect in school. My cousin drugged a person and is now fired from his job because of it," Damian said with frustration.

"No, it's Roxanne's fault Bruce was fired. We would've never gone to that club, to begin with, if she was never born. Hell, Sasha would've never even known Bruce existed if it wasn't for Roxanne," Penny said.

"If that's true, then we would've never met. We never would have started to date if it was not for Sasha and Voxy meeting Bruce. You were their friend before me, and my cousin met you," Damian said.

"Is that what you wish happened?" Damian asked.

Penny was silent momentarily.

"We never had an argument like this until Roxanne went missing. We were happy before she went missing. The moment she was gone, the whole world, our lives, and our friends' lives went to hell. She gets out of everything while we clean up the messes she left us with. She gets off scot-free because she is a victim, and we get the dump. Sasha and Bruce are victims too. And they're stuck cleaning up the mess she left behind," she says

"This isn't like you at all, my angel. Penny, why are you so angry with Voxy? I wish you would help me understand what's happening here," Damian said.

Penny just clicked her heels and started walking. Damian followed her until she went into the store's restroom. He waited outside the door for her. I heard a faint tapping nearby. I see a fly trying to go after the fluorescent lights. It might take some time. I can use this fly to go to the restroom door to listen in on Penny.

When she got angry at someone in school, she tended to vent in privet. In her venting, some pieces of truth often are found. I know it can be risky to use two illusions simultaneously. However, I am willing to try. Damian seems determined to stay by Penny's side.

I checked to make sure I was not visible to any store cameras. There are no other customers in the store besides us. I equally checked to make sure that no store employee would notice me before I began snaring the fly. The only employee I could see was a man who looked like he was in his sixties. He was reading a newspaper be hide the check-out counter. I think using two illusions is a risk worth taking to find the truth. I can also learn more about where my limits truly reside.

Looks like the coast is clear. I focused on the air around the fly and gradually took control of the fly's senses. I began feeling more comfortable seeing the fly's vision and keeping my own. The only challenge was concentrating on the first illusion alongside this new one. I felt like my control of the fly was poor compared to the last two times I tried this illusion. I reminded myself it is not the end of the world if I lose connection with the fly. It's only a test to see what I can do and check on Penny to find out what is happening.

After struggling to get the fly to the bathroom door, I hear Penny's voice muffledly. It took some time for me to focus on the fly's ability to pick up sound waves.

"Damn it, God damn it." I hear Penny say with the sound of running water.

It possibly was the sound from the bathroom sink.

"This wasn't how things were supposed to happen. This isn't how everything was supposed to play out. God damn it. Bruce was never interested in Sasha or Roxanne...." Penny said before sobbing.

"Bruce... said that he loved me before... how did this mess even happen?" Penny asked.

It was after a few moments of sobs. I hear Penny start talking again.

"He said he loved me. Before Damian, Bruce and I had a wonderful relationship. It was only for two weeks. Then, after we made love, he stopped talking to me. I thought that if I dated Damian that Bruce would get jealous and want me back. I did everything to be the perfect girlfriend to make Bruce wish he had me back. Now, he slept with Sasha. How did this happen? A girl he never loved. He would sooner sleep with her than be with me. He lost his job because of that. Damn, you, Roxanne. Your existence ruined our lives. You're the reason Sasha ordered that drink Bruce drugged. You're the reason Sasha was used by Bruce. Your birth is our despair from having happiness. I don't know where you are, but I pray it's a hell worse than this. I'm stuck in a relationship with this circus clown. I never wanted this relationship, but it happened because of you," Penney uttered.

At that point, I had enough of Penny's toxic vent. So, she got used by Bruce before dating Damian. Poor Damian doesn't have a clue he is being used by Penny. I would say that I feel sorry for her. After hearing her damn me to hell, did I find feeling sorry for her a hard thing to do. Right now, I feel sorrier for Damian. He has been used by Penny for three years. He is left wondering why his relationship with Penny may end soon. Damian and Sasha, I hope you both can find happiness after the dust settles.

"Voxy!?" I hear Damian's voice crack.

Fear ran up my spine. Did I lose focus on my visual illusion? Did he see me? Crap! Instinctively, I focused even more on my illusion to hide from Damian. Was it too late to make a difference, though?

"O', I... I'm sorry, ma'am. I didn't mean to startle you. I thought I saw a young girl beside you who looked a bit like a friend of mine. I must be imagining things. I didn't mean to bother you," Damian said.

"You did give me a bit of a fright, young man. I can understand one's eyes playing mean tricks. Happens to me plenty, especially as I get older," I said, trying to play the part of an old lady.

The man behind the counter adjusted his newspaper and got Damian's and my attention.

"Since my friend went missing, seeing things that are not there is becoming a habit. I can't even see what's happening in my relationship with my girlfriend," Damian said, sounding defeated.

"Sometimes, relationships can be hard to see. It takes work from both people to see the full picture," I said, wanting to comfort my emotionally wounded friend.

"I know that. My mother says the same thing, too. But it feels like she keeps turning away from me whenever I try to understand what she sees that I don't see. How do I get her to stay?" Damian asks.

"Sadly, young man, you can't make people stay and work problems out with you. It is up to the person fleeing the problem to come to the table of their free will for things to improve. However, that's only my opinion on the matter," I said,

I am struggling trying not to talk to him as I used to. I must be only an acquaintance now. I know I can't be involved in their lives as their friend anymore. A part of me wishes I could be there for Damian and Sasha. Perhaps as their protector, but I can't. This is all I can do for them now.

"Thank you for your honesty, ma'am. Sorry again for the fright," Damian said while seeing Penny leave the restroom.

He followed her and asked her if she was okay. I hear Penny lie, saying she is fine now and just had an upset stomach. I could only listen to Damian apologizing for being hard on her as they left. After a moment, I was about to exit the store when I heard the man behind the counter speak.

"Your control needs work, young one. I'm disappointed that you almost exposed our kind this evening," the man said while putting down his newspaper.

Looking at his face, I think I saw him briefly at the council meeting.

"I'm guessing that young man and lady were your old friends before your blood woke?" the man asked.

"Yes, I used to be their friend before I woke," I said as an old woman.

I was unsure if I should take down my illusion before him.

"The young man is a good person. The lady should consider herself lucky to have found a man that committed to her. You also seem to have been a good friend to them. If they knew what you tried to do for them, they would have the sense to thank you when the end comes for our kind," he said.

What does that mean? What a strange vampire.

"Am I in trouble then?" I ask.

"Yes, but that is for your father to decide the punishment. I'm just a humble shopkeeper," he said.

"Thank you for your honesty," I say, feeling concerned.

"A quick word of advice, young one," The man said.

"Don't try learning new skills in public. You got lucky this time, but it could've been a nightmare for us. You need to learn this lesson soon. Your actions affect us all. Be responsible with your powers," The man behind the counter explained.

I left feeling confused. I know I was scolded for my actions, but I felt respected in light of my recklessness by that shopkeeper. When I head outside, I see Amelia's bat form fly over to an alleyway on the other side of the street. I walk over and see Amelia in her human form.

"Are you positive that it is safe to transform here?" I asked Amelia.

"I'm sure," Amelia answered, pointing to the empty walls.

"Not a camera in sight," Amelia said.

"Why didn't you tell me earlier? You could've hidden here while I spied on my old friends," I blurted.

"This seemed like a good chance to test your knowledge. How can you create plans in a crisis with someone in your care? I only went along with your plan because it seemed interesting. I want to know how it would work out," Amelia said.

"Great. Did I pass your test?" I asked.

"No, Mr. Barbosa told me what happened. When I saw your friends, I knew you would want to check in on them. We're lucky that they went into Mr. Barbosa's general store. I told him by telekinesis about the situation and my proposed test for you. He agreed to keep an eye on you. He told me that your visual illusion weakened, creating a phantom form of your true appearance for a moment. Your friend saw your phantom appearance and talked to you about it. Thankfully, he wasn't suspicious and accepted the illusion. It's okay, though. That is why we gave you a haircut and new clothes. To make sure you don't look exactly like your old self for now. Even though that happened, no one would know you are you," Amelia replied.

"It's okay to fail a test you didn't know could happen. The important thing is that now you can learn from your mistakes. Father will continue to work with you, and you'll be an old pro in no time." Amelia assured me.

One step at a time. Call it pride, but I hate failing. I hate that I was being tested without knowing it. I knew I could make a mess by using more than one illusion at a time. I wouldn't know what I could truly do without an experiment. It's fine that I failed. At least, that is what I'm trying to convince myself.

7

Something Old and Something New

Along the way, neither Amelia nor I talk. She didn't even continue to talk about Germany. I would think Amelia would like to know what I found out by following my friends. However, she seems content with not saying a word. She simply was humming a tune I had never heard. The lack of curiosity for her is now starting to bother me.

"Okay, I get that you tested me. But aren't you curious about what I learned about my friends?" I ask.

"You don't want to hear this, but I have a good idea about the conversation. We spent a lot of time watching you over the last fourteen years. We investigated your friends and their families to ensure you were safe. It can't be helped.

Penny has had abandonment issues since her father divorced her mother. Since Pennies mother is a gambling addict, she is never there for Penny. Bruce is a sex addict to compensate for his low self-esteem. He grew up being chronically compared to other family members. Constantly feeling less than others, he lacks self-love. Damian is fortunate to have had a family that built a healthy work-relationship-balanced life.

You know as much as we do about Sasha. She had a young first love, longing for Bruce. It is painful when first loves don't work out. It'll hunt her for a good time that she was a rape victim. Although, I believe that women like her will become a stronger person with continued support. Sasha does have people in her life that will care for her during this time. She'll have a happier life ahead of her. Even if it might not feel that way for a spell. Damian will also recover after facing a loveless relationship. He'll be over the moon when he finds a person who truly loves him back. As for what they might have said about you, I would've given them hell if I could. However, I'll not get involved. I know you love them even though they hurt your feelings. That is why I'm not going to ask. I'll only be angry. Instead, I'll love you and affirm you," Amelia explained.

"If you know all that, why was it hard for you to understand me when I arrived?" I asked, feeling lost.

I mean, she knows more about my friends than I ever did.

"Haven't you also had some time to know me by now? I'm not dumb, but I'm not that smart, either. Unlike August and father, I don't understand politics, making laws, or how to advise people through legal matters. I don't know how to care for or teach people like Julia. I don't understand why things are the way they are. Or how to test and find out like you.

I took years to learn how to read and write in different

languages. Much longer than any other vampire would take. However, I can tinker, be brutally honest, and find ways to make things work.

Because of my work for the family, I have learned a lot about patterns over the years. One pattern I see often involves behaviors. I work with good people and scheming people every day. Humans and vampires alike while watching our clan's economic welfare. Since I work with people, I learn where to find information. Patterns form after many years of interacting with people and learning their stories. Some habits need direct involvement for change, but most don't.

No matter how long I live, the one pattern that still confuses me to this day is our family. I don't understand why Julia and August fight with each other when they do. I don't even understand why August and Julia fight with me from time to time. I don't get why father sometimes gets angry or scared when he does. Even with fourteen years of watching over you, I don't understand you. For example, I don't understand how you could make friends with humans. Or why humans would want to be friends with vampires. It's outside my wheelhouse.

The only person I could possibly understand was my mother. Yet sometimes her behavior baffles me to this day," Amelia explained with eyes looking off in the distance.

"I see. I still think it's impressive that you do know a lot about reading people's behavior. You can also tell the difference between who is a vampire and who is a human. I don't even know that much yet," I said.

"I know that father would want you to learn and practice

skills related to your new job. That is why I thought the test would help," Amelia said.

"I think we can still have fun and continue to practice working out that earlier lesson today. Want to do some more practice situations on the way back home?" I proposed.

"Trying to redeem yourself, my little sister?" Amelia asked.

"Fine. But I'm still telling father about what happened this evening," Amelia continued.

"I don't plan to hide the truth. I just want to know that I can do better than earlier. It's for the human's sake and our family's peace of mind," I explain.

"That would be helpful. Okay, more tests on the way back. But we'll need to get our errand done quickly," Amelia said, picking up her pace.

Before we knew it, both of us started to run. I have no clue where we're going. I only followed Amelia, who seemed happy to be in first place in our private race. It was only a moment when Amelia stopped at a storefront. It looked like an antique store.

"Are we picking up our errand from this store?" I asked breathlessly.

"Yep, this is the place. If we need repair work done, we can bring them back here," Amelia said while opening the door to the store.

I enter the store first. I looked around, wondering how I could tell this was where sound stones would be sold. It looked like any run-of-the-mill antique store to me. There is a thick dust coating on their goods. The store smelled of mold. Most of the woodwork has nicks and splits in them. Other wooden pieces have minor water damage. There were dolls with damaged hair wearing clothes with stains, cracked faces, or lost limbs. I kept looking around but couldn't find anything out of place. That was until Amelia told me to follow her. I did. We met a young man with a flattened nose smiling at us. The man's clothes looked as antique as everything else in this shop. Even the jeweled pendant he had on him looked antique. I started to wonder if it was a sound stone or a bloodstone. It looked somewhat like Kalt's pendant.

"Hello, Mr. Jones!" Amelia said, greeting the man with a handshake.

"Is Ms. Marry in today?" she inquired.

"Yes," Mr. Jones answered.

"I believe Ms. Marry is in the back of the shop. Would you like me to let her know you're here, Ms. Amy?" Mr. Jones asked.

I looked over at Amelia.

"If you don't mind, I would appreciate the help," Amelia replied.

Mr. Jones nodded and left us to get Ms. Marry from the back.

When he was out of earshot, I used my telekinesis to ask, 'Okay, Amelia, I have two questions for you. One, is he not a vampire?'

'No, he is human. Like many people nowadays, the whole myths and monster culture bring out the fans. As you can guess, Mr. Jones loves the idea of vampires,' Amelia replied with her telekinesis.

'Then, Ms. Marry is the actual shopkeeper? Wait, that is not my second question!' I thought.

'Yes, Ms. Marry runs the shop selling and repairing sound stones. I won't limit your questions. If you have another, go ahead and ask.' Amelia replied thoughtfully.

'Why did he call you Amy?' I wondered.

'When you live a long life in the same area, humans wonder why some people don't age. That's why changing our looks, being less social for a few years, and pretending to change store ownership helps keep humans in the dark. Giving out fake names is a part of this line of work. Julia and August don't have to worry about it as much as we do. By the way, you better come up with a nickname to give Mr. Jones if he should ask. You also might what it to be a good name. You'll have to introduce yourself by that name for at least thirty years. Then you can pick out whatever name you want to be called after that,' Amelia shared by thought.

Before I could think of my next question for Amelia, Mr. Jones returned with a woman. If she was human, it would look like she would be about the same age as Mr. Jones.

"Hello, Amy! I was expecting you. I see you have brought your sister with you," Ms. Marry said.

"Would any of you ladies like tea during your visit today?" Mr. Jones asked.

"If you don't mind, Josh, could you bring us a set with a teapot? That way, we can serve ourselves, and you don't have to fuss over us should other customers show," Marry replied for us.

"Of course, Ms. Marry. But really, who would buy an antique at this time of night?" Mr. Jones asked.

Without another word, Ms. Marry led us to the back of the store while holding both Amelia's and my hands. Going through the shop's back door felt like I was in a completely different type of store. There were display cases of jewelry covering most of the room. There wasn't a speck of dust to be found. It smelled of lemon and roses. A simple wooden table with four wooden chairs was in the middle of the room. Marry led us to the table and told us to sit while she fetched our order from storage. I feel confused. I want to ask Amelia more questions. Before I could pick a question, Mr. Jones came to our table with a tray carrying a tea set. Amelia thanked him for the hospitality. Mr. Jones bowed and told Amelia to thank Ms. Marry for being a great host before leaving.

"Here we are, Amy. It's not often we have a request like this one," Ms. Marry said, walking to the table.

Amelia took a sip from her teacup. I hadn't noticed Amelia poured tea into a cup for Ms. Marry and me. Ms. Marry put a gray box on the table. A part of me felt like I'm facing that white box with the silver ribbon again. I wonder, did Kalt order the courting stone from here?

"Something wrong dear girl?" Ms. Marry asked me.

I don't know if I should ask Mary if Kalt was here recently. I didn't know if I could handle the answer right now.

"No, I was just lost in thought. I have many questions for my sister, but it can wait until we're home," I replied.

"Well, if you have any questions, please don't hesitate to ask. I want this shop to feel welcoming. This is a new start to a new way of life for you. We want to help you enjoy this new season of your life," Ms. Marry said.

"Can we see the new amulet?" Amelia asked.

"How about we let your sister open it?" Ms. Marry asked.

I looked back at the box and felt the same dread as when I got Kalt's gift. I try to remind myself this situation is different as I open the box. I half expect to find something blue in the box. To my relief, the first color I see is red. A wave of relief came over me as I finished removing the lid.

"O' Wow!" I exclaim.

"As I said, it was an interesting request. We get a request for odd shapes since it has become the latest craze. This piece is a delicate work," Ms. Marry explained.

"What do you think, Roxanne?" Amelia asked.

"It's perfect," I replied.

I took the red musical eight-note amulet out of the box. It almost looks finer than a well-sculpted glasswork. The little details may not stand out as much, but it is still a marvel of craftsmanship.

"I'm glad you like it. Please take your time to enjoy our shop while you finish your tea. Again, if you have any questions, please feel free to ask," Ms. Marry said as she got up from her chair with her teacup.

She excused herself and left Amelia and me to talk and finish our tea.

"I can't believe it! I never would've thought of my sound stone being shaped like a musical note," I said, trying to keep my tone at a whisper.

"We might not know everything. But we know of your love for music and your mother," Amelia said plainly.

"Julia, August, and I have never been able to meet her in person. We only ever happen to see her with our father while being out. Father told us we couldn't help because he didn't want to be put in a difficult situation. He didn't want to choose between protecting her or us if caught in danger. He needed us to be able to look after each other and not get into any trouble while he watched her. So, we kept our distance until she had you. Father still wanted us to stay safe, but he also wanted us to know about you.

Your mother was a good singer. She sang to you until you went to sleep. At least that is what she did for you the first eight months we were allowed to visit secretly. We could look after you and her from a distance. After those eight months, things returned to normal for us. We let dad work and kept to ourselves. Only until your birthdays come could we visit you from a distance again. We anticipated each year, your blood would wake. Then it became just you. We watched over you more since then till now. We what you to be proud of who you are and where you come from." Amelia explained.

"Thank you, Amelia. But should we really be talking so freely here? You did say that Mr. Jones is human, right?" I said, praying Mr. Jones wasn't around to hear this conversation.

"You don't need to worry about that in this store. Ms. Marry is used to him snooping, and they're infatuated with each other. It wouldn't surprise me if he helped craft your sound stone since he's an artist," Amelia said.

"Then why have them call you...?" I started to ask.

"Amy. Because they need to help keep up the illusion for other human customers. Mr. Jones didn't know that you were my sister. He might have guessed it, but it would be concerning if he made an assumption without Ms. Marry's permission. Until you let them know how you want to be addressed, they'll only refer to you as Amy's sister. Still, he could have asked you about yourself, so I told you to start thinking of your nickname. When it has been affirmed in this store, word gets around," Amelia answered.

"I guess I'll need a nickname since I will be helping you with this type of work?" I ask.

"Yes, you really should. It will also help make things easier for you should the boy you're protecting wonder as much as your mother did," Amelia replied.

"I thought it was improper to use nicknames," I said.

"August probably told you something similar. It's improper to rely on nicknames when addressing people formally. Our sick-minded cousin never bothers to address people by their actual names if he can get by with nicknames. It takes less work to invest one's attention in people by creating names than affirming their names. However, dealing with business, we need to use nicknames for only so much time. We try not to rely on nicknames if we can get away with using our actual names. In your case, however, many human people know you as Roxanne already and are looking for you. That is why for now, you need to use a nickname for business. Also, you'll want a nickname while protecting the human gem," Amelia informed me.

"I wonder what should my nickname be?" I ask myself reflectingly while looking at my lovely new sound stone.

"Music...My mother's name was Aria," I continue pondering out loud.

I play with my new amulet while wrapping my mind around a name.

"We need to get going if you want time to redeem yourself before sunup with your training. You don't have to give Mr. Jones and Miss Marry a name now. You can let them know when you're ready," Amelia said.

Amelia pulled me out of my seat, and we headed out of the jewelry room to the antique storefront. Ms. Marry and Mr. Jones greeted us and inquired if we enjoyed our stay. Amelia told them that we did and thanked them for the wonderful tea. I also thanked them.

I was surprised when I heard Ms. Marry's voice asking, 'Have you decided how we should address you in our store, young one?'

"Cadence," I said out loud.

All three of them looked at me with surprise.

"I thought you would like to know my name since you know my sister, Amy. I'm Cadence." I said, trying to sound casual.

Mr. Jones and Ms. Marry smiled.

"It's a pleasure to meet you today, Cadence. If you should need anything from us, please feel free to visit. We're more than happy to help you and your sister Amy." Ms. Marry said sweetly.

Mr. Jones nodded.

Amelia put her arm around my shoulder and said, "We better be going now. We'll see you both in a few weeks."

With that, Amelia and I headed out the front door. I decided to wear my new amulet for the trip back home. Yet after two blocks down the street, I see a man coming out of a hotel building. The man looked familiar, but it took me a moment to recall where I saw him last. My instinct was that I was in danger. Then it hit me. He was the man who tried to follow me home from the café that one evening. I stepped back, and Amelia turned to see what had happened.

"What is it?" Amelia asked.

I couldn't bring myself to speak. I could only look at the man heading back into the hotel. Amelia followed my gaze and saw him.

"Do you know that man?" Amelia asked.

"He tried to follow me home from the café the night father returned from the Van Schlager mansion. I managed to lose him that evening with an invisibility illusion. It felt like a risk because I couldn't tell if he was a vampire or human at the time," I exclaimed.

"He's human. It looks like he's a maintenance worker for our hotel. He possibly thought you were one of our sisters or me at the time. Still, most employees don't talk with business owners. Especially with how large of a staff we have working at our hotel. You and I would only have time to talk with the general manager. Perhaps a few words to a lead manager if disciplinary action is needed. But never staff," Amelia explained.

Amelia started to make her way to the hotel entrance. I thought we would head back somewhere close to home to do some training. What is she doing now? I ended up following her into the hotel. I felt amazed by the decor. It really felt like a grand high-class place. There was gold leaf work on the walls and pillars, oversized mirrors, marble floors, and a hint of cream coloring on the walls. Amelia approached the front desk and asked the clerk for the red phone.

"I'm sorry, miss, but that phone is for employees. Guests aren't allowed to use it," The clerk said fearfully.

Amelia glared at them.

"The business owner can also use the red phone to get a hold of the general manager in an emergency. I'm one of your business owners, and I wouldn't be asking if I didn't need to speak with Mr. Crawler. Now, are you going to hand over that phone?" Amelia growled.

The poor clerk was shaking like a leaf and tried to pick up the red phone for Amelia. Yet the phone falls out of their hands and onto the floor, undamaged. It took a few tries, but the clerk picked up the phone and handed it to Amelia. I watched Amelia hit two buttons on the red phone and hold the phone close to her ear.

"Crawler, this is Amy Kurt. I strongly recommend you get down to the front desk quickly. My sister and I need to talk to you about a recent issue," Amelia said.

She hung up the phone and returned it to the clerk, who was still shaking.

"Crawler is a good man and runs a tight ship here. It's some of the other lead managers who let things slide," Amelia told me but kept her eyes on the clerk.

I can't tell if they currently fear Amelia or Mr. Crawler. It didn't take long for a hefty set man in a black tux to meet us.

"What is this recent issue, Ms. Amy?" Mr. Crawler asked.

"The recent issue involves one of the hotel's maintenance employees and my sister Cadence here. May we speak more about it in privet?" Amelia inquired.

Mr. Crawler leads Amelia and me to an employee breakroom to talk. Once we were all inside and seated, Amelia started to explain.

"About four nights ago. A man followed my little sister home from a little café called Dive-in Brews. Before I called you, my sister told me she had seen the same man who followed her from the café outside the hotel. From the clothes he was wearing, I could tell that he was one of our maintenance employees. Before you say I'm going off the rails here, I'm not suggesting anything. I just want the matter to be looked into. We have cameras around the front doors so you can see which employee we're discussing here. I would like you to check to see if the employee was at the café the night in question and if they have any recordings of him following my sister. Only if needed would I like the employee to receive a warning about stalking young women. Even if it isn't on company time, his public behavior can make guests question their safety during their stay," Amelia said.

"I hear your concern, Amy. But let's get to the heart of the matter. It's not that the employee is stalking women. It's because he had the balls to stalk one of the business owners of this hotel. Your sister, Cadence, was it?" Mr. Crawler asked.

I nod.

"I can investigate the matter if you both feel it's needed. However, the one thing I can do for you both right now is deliver a warning to the employee. Following his boss home from a café or anywhere else will not be tolerated. If it should happen again, they'll lose their job. Is this an acceptable start to addressing the incident?" Mr. Crawler continued to ask.

We both nodded in agreement.

"Then consider the warning as good as delivered. I'll find the employee and deliver the warning right now." Mr. Crawler assured us.

8

Something Borrowed and Someone's Blue Eyes

After Mr. Crawler's assurance, Amelia and I finally started on our way home.

"So that's our hotel. It's a crazy high-end place," I said.

"The man should consider himself lucky to be able to work there. We pay our maintenance people 20 dollars more per hour than the rest of the hotels in the area. We're not going to take stalking behavior lightly from any of our employees," Amelia growled.

"When you mean it's the economic gem for our family, you're not kidding. Can we afford to pay our employees that much more an hour?" I ask.

"Yes, we can afford to treat our employees well. This situation shouldn't be a problem in the future. You and the boy can feel a little safer being out and about," Amelia said.

My safety really is her priority. I'm wondering if telling

her about the stalking was the right thing to do. I just wasn't expecting to see the same man again so soon. Actually, I was hoping I would never see him again. Yet life has other plans.

"If we can change the subject to something hopefully interesting and fun. I know you wanted to show me how to turn this work into something more palpable. Like me redeeming myself from the failed test," I suggested.

"Yeah, let's go to the one park. It's close to home. Dad can find us when it's time to head back. You can show me what you would do if in danger in a place like it," Amelia replied.

She must be talking about the park August took me to show me her wolf's transformation. It would be the perfect place to hide from danger than worry about being in danger. At least, I think so. When we got to the park, Amelia proposed a situation where we were chased into a heavily wooded area. Hiding from someone's aggressive hunting dog.

"Amelia, I don't think a situation like that would happen here. There are lease laws for dogs. Even if someone's dog got loose and was aggressive, I don't think a vampire would need to do anything more than what a human would do in that situation," I said.

"Some people don't train their dogs. The instinct to hunt is natural to them. What would you do?" Amelia asked.

I sigh.

"The human would be the priority. Getting him up in a tree could distance him and the dog," I said.

"Tell me then which tree you would use for that cause?" Amelia asked.

I looked around at the trees. It's hard to see in the darkness, but after some time, I could tell it was a trick question. None of the trees had low-hanging limbs. Not even a grown man could reach, let alone climb, to the lower branch of any of the trees.

"I see. Climbing is out of the picture. Being close to the ground is dangerous, too," I replied.

"So, what would you be able to do?" Amelia asked.

"He would need to keep moving, but that could be challenging for him here. I could use a snare on the dog, but there is still a chance that the dog wouldn't be easily influenced. An invisibility illusion would do nothing to hide our smell from a dog. What else is there?" I wondered out loud.

"It's not a bad problem to have if you have family nearby," I hear father's voice say near the entrance to the park.

"Our ability to use telekinesis is key to most problems we face. Amelia, that was a clever problem to pose to your sister. It's based on a past incident in German," father continued to say.

"What happened?" I asked.

"I was chased by a hunting dog into the woods once. I tried to get away but wasn't very good at my transformations. I ran till I could run no more. I ended up sending out a cry with my telekinesis hoping for someone to help, and father showed up as a wolf and ran off the dog," Amelia said.

"You're still to young to challenge a dog head-on now, Roxanne. When you get older, you'll have more options about handling danger," father said.

"For now, I think learning to find places and people in our clan to help is your most powerful asset for that boy. I can understand wanting to show your strength and cunning, but true skill and wit come with time. You can also send the boy a wrong impression of who you are and what you are capable of by not acknowledging the need for help," father explained.

I couldn't help but reflect on my day. Amelia had people keep an eye on me and requested help for me. To keep me safe while I spied on my old friends. People who are able and willing to fix essential tools. People who have strong relationships with beings on both sides of life. Also, people who are determined to maintain peace and order when threats show themselves. We met a lot of people today. Humans and vampires alike, and Amelia relied on them to do what was right without once denying her own strength.

"I think I do understand that better after today. Amelia was strong and still placed a lot of trust in others to do what was right. It helped play an important part in keeping our clan's secret safe," I replied to father.

Amelia smiled.

Then something dawned on me that I hadn't wondered till now.

"Wait a minute! During the days our father was at the Van Schlager mansion dealing with Kalt's inappropriate gift of a courting stone, you and the others told me we had a problem with clan members. It would be bad to draw attention to the fact that father was away. If members are willing to work with us and keep an eye on me, why did you tell me that?!" I asked.

"Two reasons," Amelia started, "We wanted to know more about you. We wanted to know how you thought and planned considering your new life. How would you adapt to our world, which may be safer but not always safe?"

"And the other?" I asked.

"It was to test some of our clan members who lived nearby to keep an eye on you. After what you told me today, they didn't do a good job of that one time you had a human stalker," Amelia replied.

I took a moment to let it all set in. I was never in any real danger except that one time. I had never expected my sisters to have their own ways of keeping watch, even in times like that. They're something else to let me think we were in danger.

"Amelia has had time to work on those relationships with our clan members. A few are willing to work with the family and help keep the peace. However, some members are unwilling to help or work with us. They might even try to take advantage of whatever they can with any opportunity. For now, it's good for you to meet people we trust and start working on building relationships with them. They would be your allies if something was to happen. As you meet more people, you'll find more people willing to work with you that may not want to work with your sisters or me. Be open to forming healthy relationships with our clan members, for the boy's and your sake," father advised.

"I think I'm ready to head back home and kick up my feet," Amelia said while stretching.

"I thought you were going to tell father what happened today," I said.

"I can do that inside," Amelia said.

"O', What happened today?" father asked.

Amelia waited until we were inside before telling father about our day. He was unhappy that I got spotted by Damian while spying on him and Penny. He was glad I was safe, our secret didn't get out, and I learned an important lesson. August and Julia decided to reflect on what they'd do if they were in the same situation. Father used that time to talk to me more through telekinesis.

'Illusions work much like your mind. If one works on two different tasks at the same time, problems can happen in both. The same can be said for working on two different illusions simultaneously. Nothing productive or effective will happen when you work on more than one at a time. The only exception to that rule is if the illusions are similar and work collectively on the same goal. It will require a lot of concentration on your part. As you continue to learn new talents take your time building concentration. When you become an immortal vampire like me, you'll be able to control more than one illusion at a time. It will take a lot of practice to become effective at it,' father thoughtfully reminisced.

I felt hopeful that someday I could be able to do more. Right now, though, I'm limited in what I can do. So far, I keep messing up plans to keep the boy and me safe. I feel like a part of me is missing. What I can do. What I can't do. It's all still a mystery. I'm told that I am strong and have unique gifts. Yet I can't make the most of my strength and talent. I need help. I need answers. I need to keep looking for some kind of clue to help me better understand just who I am in this mess.

I thanked my family for my new sound stone and listened to tells of their day. According to August, the sub-council had decided for a clan leader's oldest child to have the honor of becoming a parent. August thinks that they want to offer the option to Julia and Cronos. Still, they would also consider allowing me the opportunity if Julia and Cronos wish to wait. I told my family it's best to leave the option for Julia and Cronos. August continued by explaining that it doesn't need to be decided on this year. The option will remain available to us if we want it.

Before we knew it, it was time for bed. I'm starting to think that the child in my dreams could've been my mind playing tricks. Perhaps for one night, I could sleep like an average person. Right now, all I have is dreamless sleep. That night was no exception.

The next few days have been crazy. I had lessons with my father and was given more books on illusions to read when I wasn't packing my room for our coming move. While I pack, I still try to send bugs around the house to find the place I used to hide, but to no avail. I found an old, worn book hiding in the walls. One dawn, I crept out of my room to see if I could move the wood framing to get the book free. It took some time. Eventually, I got the book out of the wall without damage. I tried to read the book when I could find the time.

It appears to be my mother's journal. What I have read from it so far talks about when and how she met my father. Some of her antics that father told me about early are in there. As interesting as the book seemed, it felt like mother didn't know what it meant for her to be seen by vampires as a gem. She didn't feel powerful or that she could make anything special happen. She just loved to sing. I can't help but feel the same way. I'm probably just as foolish too. Foolish for experimenting at inappropriate times. Yet I don't feel I have time to reflect on such things.

I've been working on illusions with the family when I'm not packing or studying. Learning how we manage the clan's businesses from Amelia. They even taught me how to transform into a bat.

That is quite the story. To sum it up, I can transform into a bat fine since I have learned to become a wolf with no problem. Flying as a bat is unnatural for me. I fell to the ground more times than I can count. It's much different than when I snare a fly or moth. There's more physical work involved that I'm not used to doing.

Amelia still tests me on how I would solve surviving some possible danger with a human beside me. The first question I learned to ask Amelia is, "Who from our clan do we trust lives or works around here?"

Amelia would then tell me who I should consider contacting with telekinesis. We've taken the time to meet Amelia's acquaintances and friends. With so many people to meet and remember, I admit that I can't help but feel confused. I'm not sure who I know and who I don't know. When we get home, Amelia tests me with a map to tell her where she lives and works. Some nights I can only remember half of the people. Though Amelia works with me till I can remember all the new and older acquaintances we've met.

We were close to finishing packing the house when father advised me to take some time to be on my own today.

"It's been a while since your last hunt. You know our

territory well enough now. Where to go and who to ask for help. We can't let you rely too much on your sound stone to do all the work. I think you should be able to manage a hunt independently," father said.

I felt surprised and almost fearful at the thought that no one would be around to help me. Although it was what I wanted. I didn't want to rely on my family too much. I was not expecting them to let me try so soon.

"Are you sure you trust me to be on my own for a hunt? I could mess up," I said.

"You might, but I don't believe you will. You've been working on your illusions and transformations every day. You've been meeting and started working with our family friends. On that note, I have faith that you have more chances to succeed," father assured me.

I thanked him for letting me have a chance to do things alone this evening. Amelia was upset that she couldn't spend time with me today but understood why. Julia and August tried to act mature and as assuring as our father. Still, they couldn't hide their anxiety despite the words of encouragement. It felt like all three of my sisters were holding their breath. Wanting in silence to go well for me today. I understand why. They have been beside me for weeks and know I still have much to learn. I feel that way myself. Nevertheless, I do need to grow a little more independent.

After breakfast and getting ready for the day, I started out for a hunt. I really didn't plan where I would like to go. I would love to see and talk with Sasha. Yet if I messed up talking to Sasha like I did with Damian, I may not have someone around to help clean up my mess. I also want to be able to check on my Aunt Madeline and Uncle Ernest. They don't live in our territory, though. From what I've been told, they live on the line far north between three territories. The Sturm territory, The Van Schlager territory, and our territory. None of the clans can govern it because it's on the edge of all three. It's one of the few neutral zones.

On top of that, their house in the neutral zone is closer to Van Schlager's territory than ours. I could go there, but I wouldn't have anyone to help if anything happened. I'm already creating enough worry for my family. I think that I need to just keep my head down today. Someday, I hope I can check on my aunt and uncle. It can't be today.

I think a park, like Riggy Park, is nearby in our territory and that neutral zone. I think it's called Clear Peak Park. It doesn't draw as big of a crowd, but they still have entertainment. I can feel close to where my aunt and uncle live even if I can't see them yet. I make my way over to Clear Peak Park.

I ate like I did my first night as a vampire during the trip. I'm thankful I don't need to worry about food as I used to. With my sound stone, I have peace I didn't have before. I still had an occasional drink making a passing comment. I was also stopped by a lost woman looking for her house.

I ended up helping her to a nearby police station. I explained to the lady that she needed to tell the nice people in the office what she had told me. I tried to explain that the people in the building could do more to help her than I could. It seemed to take some back and forth. Eventually, she got tired of talking with me and went into the building for help.

At least someone in there should be able to help her. Getting a thank you would have been nice, but I shouldn't expect thanks nowadays. I need to stay in the shadows and not get involved in human lives as much. That thought saddens me.

When I got to the park, I felt some happiness again. The music was cheerful. There were small conversations among couples and children. I knew the venues were smaller, yet I still felt like a lost face in a crowd. Good eating and enjoying this time in peace should be easy for me. I started my feeding trance, and it felt natural to me. I felt like I could eat more in less time. I wonder if it's because of all my constant training these last few days. My body is becoming used to the flow of living energy that it's starting to feel more like second nature.

Before I could dwell more on why eating soundly and deeply felt more effortless, I heard a familiar voice nearby that broke my concentration.

"O' my, O' my! My love's gem of a sister is here!" I hear Cronos's voice say.

I turn my head to find them in the crowd. When I saw them, I noticed another person walking next to Cronos.

"Cronos! It's good to see you. What brings you here?" I asked.

"What did you forget already, little gem? I told you and your family I would move in with you all soon. And I told you I would bring a friend when I do," Cronos said.

"O', I thought that was going to happen after we moved back to our old family's home," I replied.

I looked at Cronos's guest and said, "Then that would mean your Gabriel?"

The man looked over at me and nodded.

"Yes, I'm Gabriel Maxwell, miss," Gabriel said awkwardly.

He didn't seem comfortable making any eye contact with me. It felt like a shame that I couldn't see the rest of his eyes. I can only see his right eye. It's a delicate deep blue color. He kept looking at the stage where a couple performed a folk song. He had a duffel bag and a guitar case in one hand. His clothes seemed worn with patches and hung loose on his frame.

"My name is Cadence," I said.

"Lovely. I feel that you'll have to tell us more about the latest news on our way to your home," Cronos said to help end the conversation.

"Now, my dear gem of a sister. Where art thou, lovely sister of yours?" Cronos asked.

"Back at my mother's home packing, my dear love-struck sibling-in-law," I teased.

"Then wilt thou show us the way to your mother's home, dear one?" Cronos asked.

"Only if thou will stop talking like this on the way there," I answered.

"Art thou truly bothered by old English? I can't help but find it romantic," Cronos teased back.

"You know that. I appreciate your love for the dramatic, Cronos. It's more amusing when it's for my sister than with me," I replied.

"I can respect that," Cronos said.

"Still, we can have some fun on the way back to my loves residence," Cronos said playfully.

"Perhaps," I replied.

"I would like to know what you've been up to these last few weeks, too," I said, inviting a conversation.

Cronos told us what he could do in code while we walked back home. Gabriel still didn't seem able to join in the conversation. He remained silent during the walk back to the house. I couldn't help but wonder if he could follow along even a part of what we said. I'm sure some of it is strength forward. A few words will become confusing without context. I also can't help but wonder how much he already knows about our vampire world.

It was not long before we got home. We spotted Julia waiting at the front door. She waved to us when she saw us coming.

"Your lady love missed you, Cronos," I said.

"I can see that. Excuse me, but I have a fair lady to meet," Cronos said, running off to meet Julia at the door.

It was sweet to see until I noticed I was alone with a silent and timid Gabriel. This was uncomfortable. I have no idea how to talk to him.

"You probably notice that we don't talk about things clearly on the way here. I will be able to help explain when we are inside. If you have anything that you would like to know, feel free to ask. My family is very caring and wants to help as able," I said.

I want Gabriel to feel more comfortable around us.

9

Tempting Song

Amelia took Cronos and Gabriel's bags when we walked into the house. She went upstairs to put them away. While Julia and I led them to the living room, where my father was. We saw my father standing by the fireplace as we entered the living room. He was feeding logs to the fire.

"Looks like one of my children is missing to greet you both," my father said warmly to our guest.

"Where is our darling, August, this evening?" Cronos asked.

"She is out on patrol this evening," my father replied.

"If I'm not mistaken, Cronos, your father has your oldest brother doing the same, right?" father inquired.

"He goes on patrols once a month. Some months he doesn't patrol at all," Cronos answered.

"I see. Regular patrolling can give some vampires the impression that a territory isn't safe. Since most vampires want to toe the line, patrolling isn't always necessary in many territories. Other vampires find it calming to know that a leader is involved and wants to look after them," father reflected aloud.

"I'm sure little August is learning a lot from doing her rounds," Cronos said.

"True. It doesn't matter how old one gets. We all can still learn something new each day," father replied with a smile and hugged Cronos.

"This person beside you must be Gabriel," father inquired.

Gabriel, who was previously scanning the living room, now looked over to face my father. He looked like he wanted to find a place to hide. Looking at the situation, dad seems a bit more intimidating when standing. Thinking back to my first night, the space felt calmer and more welcoming. Now with the packed boxes and dad standing beside the fireplace, this doesn't feel as welcoming. The room felt serious and cold.

Gabriel nodded.

"Please don't mind Gabriel's silents. He doesn't talk much when meeting new people. I promise you, after being around the family, he will start to open up more," Cronos assured us.

"You have gone through many changes in one evening," Julia said to Gabriel sympathetically.

She continued, "Even our youngest sister Roxanne had quite a time adjusting after her blood woke this year."

"I'm sorry, but who is Roxanne?" Gabriel asked.

The room fell silent, and everyone was looking at Gabriel.

"... That would be me," I said.

Only after responding did it dawn on me that I had only

introduced myself as Cadence to him. I haven't gotten around to telling him my real name.

"I'm sorry. I forgot that I told you my nickname at the park. My real name is Roxanne. Like my family told you, my vampire blood woke up this year. Before I became a vampire, I lived as a human till some weeks ago. Since some people remember me as a human who just vanished from the face of the world, I need to hide. I made a few changes and need to use a nickname outside of the house. At least for a few years until I become a memory," I said, flustered.

"Which park did you go to this evening?" Amelia asked.

"Don't worry, Amelia, I didn't go near Riggy Park. I decided to see Clear Peak Park this evening," I replied.

"Then I take it you two took a long way coming over and met Roxanne at the park," father reasoned.

"Yep, I wanted to show Gabriel the border where our families' territories meet. I also wanted to show Gabriel where Roxanne's old preschool was back when she was human," Cronos said.

"Why?" Amelia and Julia asked simultaneously.

I wanted to ask the same thing. It might be because the Sturm family wanted me to meet Gabriel for a long time. Gabriel probably knew some things about me already. The problem is it's hard to know what he knows already.

"Well, we have been telling Gabriel for years that we think he would be good friends with the late Lady Aria's daughter Roxanne," Cronos answered.

"Clearly, telling him about Roxanne had helped," Amelia replied sarcastically.

"It has helped," Gabriel said, "I'm just not fully mentally here this evening to talk properly. Sorry if I'm making a poor first impression."

Father walked over to Gabriel and put a hand on his shoulder.

"Your fine Gabriel, this evening hour isn't meant for humans to be awake. Even as a performer, you still need a good night's sleep. We can talk more tomorrow evening," my father said.

Father took his hand off Gabriel's shoulder as we heard the sound of the front door opening and closing.

"Man, is it getting even colder out there? I wish it would just snow already. Cold for the sake of chilly nights is such a pain," August said as she entered the living room.

When August saw Cronos, she ran over to hug them.

"You're here!" August sang with joy.

"It's good to see you too, beautiful future sister of mine," Cronos sang back.

"Cronos didn't come alone, August," Julia said.

"O' the human is here too," August said as she started to search the room.

When she saw Gabriel, she retracted her hug on Cronos and straightened herself out.

"It's nice to finally meet you, Gabriel," August said with an outstretched hand.

"Same here," Gabriel said, shaking August's hand.

"Since you mentioned feeling out of sorts, Gabriel, you can go to bed now. Julia will show you to the room you and Cronos will be sharing," father said.

Do they have their own room? But this is a four-bedroom house? Each of us has our own privet room. What room is he talking about? I looked over at Julia and used my telekinesis.

'What room are they using?' I wondered with Julia.

'We only figured out the sleeping arrangements today. I'm sorry I forgot to tell you when you got back. It was decided to let them use your bedroom tonight. You'll sleep with Amelia. We'll be moving to the family mansion tomorrow, so you can return to sleeping in your own room then.' Julia thoughtfully explained.

'Shit! Are you for real!?' I reflect in a mental panic

'What's wrong? I thought you'd be happy to be able to spend some more time with Amelia?' Julia pondered.

'No, I do like being able to spend more time with my sisters. I was just not expecting this.' I tried to think straight without letting more swear words rise in my train of thought.

Before another thought could be shared, Julia led Gabriel to my room. I know that I hid my mother's journal before I left. It was a good place. I wanted to read more of it this evening, but now I can't. If I try to go after it, my family will know I found it. It's not that I wouldn't tell them I had found it. I was just waiting to tell them after I finished reading it all. It could have been a clue to help me find out what happened to my mom that day. Possibly a hint as to where I had hidden in this house too. Crap, my luck.

"Hold on a moment, dear. I want Gabriel to see this real fast before going to bed." Cronos said, stirring me from my thoughts.

"Roxanne, can you transform into your wolf form real fast?" Cronos asked.

"I guess?" I replied.

Seeing Cronos' face, I could tell this wasn't an idea made a spur of the moment. Cronos' face beamed with delight.

"Cub, please!" Cronos sang with delight.

I started my transformation into a cub. I heard Cronos cheer when I was finished.

"That was much quicker than the last time I saw you change into a cute cub!" Cronos said while picking me up from the floor.

"Here, Gabriel! Just look at this cutie! Want to hold her?!" Cronos asked with joy.

Before Gabriel could respond, Cronos placed my cub form in Gabriel's arms. I feel Gabriel's body start to shake, and his heart races. The shaking is making me feel uncomfortable. I want to be put down now. I don't feel safe like this. August collects me from Gabriel's arms.

"Are you feeling better, Roxanne?" August asks.

Thank you, August. I feel safer now. I know that it's hard to know how to hold a cub. Even Julia had to teach Cronos a few weeks ago with me.

"That's true," Julia said, "I think Roxanne doesn't want you to worry about what happened, Gabriel. It's not every day you get to hold a wolf cub. Roxanne feels safer in her cub form with family since we're a pack of wolfs."

"I see. I also don't think it helps to be tired on top of that," Gabriel said.

"Sorry, gems. I was excited and wanted Gabriel to enjoy Roxanne's cub form as much as I did," Cronos said.

"It's alright. Perhaps another time when I'm less tired, and Roxanne feels safer around me," Gabriel replied.

With that, Gabriel left with Julia to my room. August put me down on the floor so I could better change back into a human form. Then Cronos, father, and August started talking politics and plans for keeping Gabriel safe between our families' two territories. All I could think about was my mother's journal. I wish I could be in bed and read more of it than having to listen to this conversation. I wonder if I could sneak away. I noticed how focused the three of them became on their discussion. Amelia seemed as bored as I was. Well... at least for a moment. The only concern is running into Julia. I could hide from her if I used an invisibility illusion. An illusion could also help me get the book out of my room while the boy sleeps. Then I can hide it in Amelia's room to read when she's asleep.

I decided it was worth a try. I quietly left the room and created a sound barrier around the stairs to prevent any sound of wood creaking from being heard. When I got upstairs, I moved the sound barrier to the hallway. To my surprise, the door to my room was open, and the light was on. As I approached my room, I could hear a faint strumming sound coming from inside. He's not asleep! Now what? After a minute of frustration, I noticed something about the notes being strummed. It sounds familiar, but I can't place the tune. It's nothing that I remember hearing growing up with my aunt and uncle. It's nothing that my friends listen to either.

What song is this? Curiosity got the best of me. I peeked into my room. I did my best to keep close to the shadows. I see Gabriel with an electric guitar in his lap. He's strumming notes while looking at ... my mother's journal! Fuck, he found it! I thought I hid it well enough that no one could see it.

"How did you find that?" the question came out of my mouth without a thought.

Gabriel's lifted his head up and looked in my direction. I tried to hide, but it was too late. He saw me.

"Roxanne? You can come in if you would like. I want to ask you whose book this is?" Gabriel said.

I didn't dare move.

"Look, if you tell me whose book this is, I will tell you how I found it, deal?" Gabriel asked.

"Fine," I replied.

I walked into the room and sat on the bed next to Gabriel. It stings to know that I messed up another simple stealth mission.

"The book is my mother's journal. My family doesn't know that I found it. I was planning to tell them about it after I finished reading it. That's why I was hiding it between the stack of boxes you when through," I explained.

"I wouldn't have noticed it was there if my guitar case didn't knock over a box of clothes. Sorry about that. I did pick up the mess I made. I promise that everything is back in the box. Why would you keep your mother's journal from your family?" Gabriel asked.

"That wasn't what we agreed to," I reminded him.

"How can I know I can trust your family if you don't trust them with this book?" Gabriel wonders out loud.

"I see you know how to play with people. Fine, the last thing I want to do is give you the impression that my family can't be trusted. I didn't tell them about it because I was trying to find out how she died. My father told me what he knew but was not there when it happened. According to him, it must have happened during the day. I can't remember anything about it since I was four years old. My father told me that he found me hiding in a clever place. The problem is I didn't know where such a place would be in this house. That is why I was looking for clues and found this book. I haven't finished going through it yet. I haven't told them because I don't want to drag them into my personal inquiries over the past. They're super supportive. I would feel guilty if they took more time away from what they needed to do. Just to support me in wanting to solve this mystery of what happened to her," I said, wishing that I didn't.

Gabriel looked at me with a softer look in his eyes. I feel myself flinch. I don't want his pity. I want him to feel safe with us and let me continue to read my mother's journal in peace. That's it.

I look down at the journal page Gabriel was focused on a moment ago. It has a handmade music sheet with notes inside. There are all kinds of notes, but X's are where some notes would be.

"What are those Xs?" I ask.

"I'm not sure. I thought the Xs were music notes. That's why I got out my guitar. I wanted to see if and how the X's would sound, but it doesn't flow or compliment the other notes. Here, give it a listen for yourself," Gabriel said.

Then he started to strum the notes on the guitar again. I listen intently. Again, I have heard this song before. Like Gabriel said, the X's don't feel like they're the right notes placed in the right spot.

"Can you stop for a moment? Do you also have a pen on you?" I ask.

Gabriel nodded. He pulled a pen from his guitar case's front pocket and handed it to me. I thanked him and opened the pen. I looked at the first X on the page and asked Gabriel to play that first part around that X again. He does. I listen to the rise and fall of the notes. The X is on a B, but the sound of the melody in my head, when he gets to that part of the song, tells me it's an E flat that last one and a half beats. I make a note of this in the book. Gabriel stared.

"Do... do you want me to try playing that instead of the X?" He asked.

I nod.

Gabriel sighs and starts from the beginning. When he gets to the part of the song, this time with the fixed note, we hear my father's voice ask, "What are you two doing?"

The look on my father's face was pale.

"We found this old journal with music in it. We're just trying to figure the X-out notes," Gabriel said.

"It's mother's journal. She mostly wrote about when you to met, and we found her song here a moment ago. I didn't know she wrote music, too," I said to help calm my father.

It did not seem to help.

"She didn't write any original music. That song fragment is as old as time itself. It's part of a song we vampires fear and respect because we don't understand it. Roxanne, you have heard the expression 'holy song' at some point since your blood woke up. We, vampires, might not mind much regarding human religions. Still, we do have our own beliefs and stories of wonder. That song fragment has an old story attached to it that we do believe and take seriously. It's believed that during the transformation of the first vampires, the song of eternity, born of life and death, created the living energy we vampires need to survive. Since the song gave birth to all vampires, we believe it would only be heard clearly again when the world we know ends. Some think the song will give us vampires a new birth to have our humanity restored again. Others believe that the song will make us something worse than monsters. We can't take that chance, child. I must ask you to let me take your mother's book. You can sing any song to your heart's content Roxanne. The same goes for you, Gabriel. Except neither of you can afford to play this song. The risk of putting innocent lives in danger is too great if the eternal song is played."

A great wave of shame came over me. Is it because my father was one of the first humans transformed that he knows the song of eternity? Is it because of me possibly being an immortal vampire like him I feel familiar with the old song?

"Did you ask her to X out some notes when she wrote the song?" I ask.

"I didn't. Thankfully, it seems your mother couldn't hear all the notes. I didn't know she had come close to knowing this song fragment. And writing it out in her journal. It's a blessing she didn't. It's rare for a person to hear even a part of the song of eternity. Even the best-trained human and vampire ear cannot hear all the notes of the song clearly. Your mother likely only wrote out what she could in hopes of uncovering the missing notes," father said sorrowfully.

"Is it possible that she died because someone knew she could hear part of the song?" I asked.

"Perhaps. Many vampires, such as myself, feel the song will only bring pain. Others would've encouraged her if they knew. Probably would've gone out of their way to keep her safe if they knew," father replied.

We spent a moment in silence. I pondered this. My father looks serious. He's not lying about the possible pain, attack, or aid that knowledge of this song would bring. She likely didn't die because of this. I can't help but wonder how and when she heard the song of eternity.

Father asked for my mother's journal to be handed over to him. I hesitated before I asked Gabriel for the book, and he handed it to me. I then gave it to my father. He thanked Gabriel and me for giving him the book. He told me to get ready for bed and advised Gabriel to rest since Cronos was also preparing for sleep. I say good night to both of them and head to Amelia's room. She was lying in bed and asked me what had happened. I told her that I would tell her about it tomorrow evening. Right now, I think I need some rest to process everything I learned today.

To be continued in Shadows Sing Vol.3.

10

A Brief Tale of Vampire Lore: The First Soul Who Didn't Want to Die

(Warning for the horror story to follow with violence, death, and cannibalism.)

(Note: The brief lore section is to tell the stories of specific family traumas that gave birth to beyond skills some vampires possess. It is only to add more insight and history to the world of Shadows Sing. It's not a required part of the read for those who don't wish to continue this section. Readers beyond this point have been warned.)

Once upon a time. While the world was young, a human gave birth to two sons. One son grew up powerful and zealous. The other is feeble and slow. Their mother wasn't attached to either of them. She left them to survive a wild world on their own the moment one of them could walk. Consequently, the feeble child is abandoned by both mother and brother. He spends his days lying by a tree root. Waiting. His movements and energy were limited. He didn't know how to feed himself.

During that time, the slow boy became self-aware. He noticed more life in his little body after sleep. He also felt energy come back into his body when he put odds and ends in his mouth. Anything that went to or from the tree he could reach was fair game. Most of the time, he felt life come back into his body. So mindful of life, this boy. Who became weaker with each passing day. He had one wish. I don't ever want this life to leave me. I don't want to die.

One day, when the boy was scared that his life was leaving him for good, he gestured for food. A wild bird drops a branch of tiny wild berries at that exact moment. The boy began to eat. When the bird flew around to return for the berries, it started falling. Seeing the bird not moving, the boy went to the bird. Seeing the bird had no life left in its body, the boy ate it. The slow boy slept well with a full belly. The next day when the boy felt hungry, a new wild bird brought him berries. This continued for days after. If a bird didn't return with food, it died.

As the boy grew into a man, other animals would bring food or wild game. If they didn't have food, they would die before him. In this, the slow man always had something to eat.

Then one day, a human found the slow man resting by the tree. This human was a hunter and charged after him with a spear. After all, the hunter was only abiding by the natural laws of the world at that time. Kill to survive. The slow man made a sound that caused the hunter to stop his pursuit. The hunter obeyed the slow man's will and dropped his weapon. The slow man made another sound, and the hunter picked up the slow man and carried him back to a cave.

The slow man found more humans in the cave. One person tried coming close to the slow man after being placed on the floor. The slow man made a sound, but the human didn't listen. Before they could reach him, they dropped dead. The slow man, seeing the human's corpse, went and ate it. As he had done with every animal corpse. This filled the others with fear. They wouldn't go near the slow man unless a sound from his mouth made them come to him and hunt for him. The one hunter who brought him to the cave often carried the slow man. The slow man and the other humans ate well.

Then one sunny day, the slow man went with his hunters on their hunt and found a strong man hunting a sabretooth tiger.

Seeing the strong man as victorious and tired, the slow man ordered the hunters to kill the strong man and collect the food. They attacked. The strong man killed the slow man's hunters. The strong man had a look of death in his eyes. The sight of death filled the slow man with fear. The slow man had his hunter put him down to finish the strong man while the slow man tried to run away. The only thought in the slow man's mind was the same as it always was. I want to live.

The slow man didn't see the strong man coming for him. For the strong man was no longer a strong man. He was a wild beast. The beast killed the slow man. The blood of the slow man covered the wounded beast. The will of the slow man lived on in the strong man who expected death. Yet death didn't come for the strong man. For what neither man knew was that they were brothers. They'll forever live in one body for the rest of their unnatural lives. The will to live was too strong, and the madness to kill ran deep.

The end.

Author's message:

Hello every lovely gem,

Your willingness to support my story, Shadows Sings, fills me with joy. Volume one of this series was the first book I have ever published. You don't know that it was an uphill battle to finish that first book during that time. By the fifth chapter, I was facing a personal and spiritual crisis. I confidently started my writing journey and found appropriate resources for editing accommodations. Hoping that I can be understood and finally be able to tell my own stories despite my learning disability of being dyslexic. While working on the discussion between Julia and Roxanne while she was cutting Roxanne's hair, I was given an inhumane criticism about my writing. I felt devastated and broken in more ways than one. I found it challenging even to touch the book I've been working on without feeling overwhelmed by my emotions. Music ended up being a source to help me let out my anger and enable me to concentrate on letting the story be what it is. During the time, I listened to many alternative and punk-rock music along with a particular new indie artist who became better know after playing Among US on Youtube.

I finished writing the book before I had to meet those critics in person. When I did, I finally felt like I had a slight sense of triumph over the comments made. It wasn't long after that I questioned whether it was worth taking the time to finish editing and publish the story. During that time, I got to hear a YouTuber's perception of the new favorite artist of mine at the time and listen to his most recent song. That song and his story encouraged me to go ahead and finally pursue the publication of the first vol. of Shadows Sing. Sorry things have been complicated when it came to writing side stories. I was becoming more concerned about leaking spoilers. So, I hope the book delay isn't too long for my dear readers.

The reason that I'm telling you this personal story is to try to help show something that I've learned from other authors. Often it's the people in our lives that we both know and don't know who has the most significant impact on helping us find the courage to pursue our dreams. I hope my stories might help encourage others who are scared or feel unable to try their best and always embrace who they are. My time in CPE (clinical pastoral education) might have helped me find desire to live authentically. Still, the courage of others living their dreams reminds me to live my dream of writing a telling stories.